W9-CYS-637

A PLUME BOOK

SALAAM, PARIS

KAVITA DASWANI is the author of *For Matrimonial Purposes* and *The Village Bride of Beverly Hills* (both available from Plume). She has been a fashion correspondent for CNN, CNBC Asia, and *Women's Wear Daily*, has written for the *Los Angeles Times* and the *International Herald Tribune*, among many other publications, and has been the fashion editor for the *South China Morning Post* in Hong Kong. A native of Bombay, she now lives in Los Angeles.

Praise for Kavita Daswani

"The culture-clash dilemmas ring heartbreakingly true."
—Entertainment Weekly

"Completely engrossing—the perfect blend of real-life drama and fairy-tale whimsy." —Jennifer Weiner, author of *Good in Bed*

"What's nice about Daswani's storytelling is her ability to maintain a light tone without sacrificing genuine sympathy for every one of her characters." *—The Baltimore Sun*

"Fairy-tale fun bursts from the confines of an arranged Indian marriage in this delectable follow-up to *For Matrimonial Purposes* . . . should appeal to readers hungering for Lahiri lite or a subcontinental Jane Green."
—Publishers Weekly

"A thoughtful romantic comedy about a young couple's first year of marriage . . . There's plenty of Hollywood glamour, but ultimately the heart of this winning novel lies in how [the couple] grow in their marriage."
—Booklist

"The ultimate beach read . . . funny, fresh . . . It's *Sex and the City* . . . with saris and samosas." *—Seattle Weekly*

"Daswani can make readers shriek with laughter. Save this enchanting novel for an uncrowded beach . . . Delightful." *—USA Today*

"A cross-cultural confection." *—People*

"A charming debut novel . . . *Bridget Jones's Diary* with a distinct Indian flavor." *—Library Journal*

"*My Big Fat Greek Wedding* meets *Sex and the City* with a curry twist."
—The Boston Phoenix

ALSO BY KAVITA DASWANI

For Matrimonial Purposes
The Village Bride of Beverly Hills

Salaam, Paris

KAVITA DASWANI

A PLUME BOOK

PLUME
Published by Penguin Group
Penguin Group (USA) Inc., 375 Hudson Street, New York, New York 10014, U.S.A.
Penguin Group (Canada), 90 Eglinton Avenue East, Suite 700, Toronto, Ontario,
Canada M4P 2Y3 (a division of Pearson Penguin Canada Inc.)
Penguin Books Ltd., 80 Strand, London WC2R 0RL, England
Penguin Ireland, 25 St. Stephen's Green, Dublin 2, Ireland (a division of Penguin
Books Ltd.)
Penguin Group (Australia), 250 Camberwell Road, Camberwell, Victoria 3124,
Australia (a division of Pearson Australia Group Pty. Ltd.)
Penguin Books India Pvt. Ltd., 11 Community Centre, Panchsheel Park,
New Delhi – 110 017, India
Penguin Books (NZ), cnr Airborne and Rosedale Roads, Albany, Auckland 1310,
New Zealand (a division of Pearson New Zealand Ltd.)
Penguin Books (South Africa) (Pty.) Ltd., 24 Sturdee Avenue, Rosebank,
Johannesburg 2196, South Africa

Penguin Books Ltd., Registered Offices: 80 Strand, London WC2R 0RL, England

First published by Plume, a member of Penguin Group (USA) Inc.

First Printing, July 2006
10 9 8 7 6 5 4 3 2 1

Copyright © Kavita Daswani, 2006
All rights reserved

℗ REGISTERED TRADEMARK—MARCA REGISTRADA

LIBRARY OF CONGRESS CATALOGING-IN-PUBLICATION DATA

Daswani, Kavita, 1964–
    Salaam, Paris / Kavita Daswani.
      p. cm.
    ISBN 0-452-28746-4 (trade pbk.)
    1. Arranged marriage—Fiction. 2. Women, East Indian—Fiction. 3. Muslim
women—Fiction. 4. Models (Persons)—Fiction. 5. Paris (France)—Fiction. I.
Title.
    PS3604.A85S25 2006
    813'.6—dc22
                                                                      2005036548

Printed in the United States of America
Set in Cochin

In memory of my dearest grandfather,
Dialdas Verhomal Daswani, with whose
blessings all things are possible.

My sincerest thanks to Aimee Taub, my editor at Plume, for always being so gracious and for having such tremendous instincts about the characters on a page and the world they inhabit.

And to Jodie Rhodes, who is tenacious and smart and kind—everything an agent should be.

And to everyone at Penguin, for their faith in me.

Salaam,
Paris

PROLOGUE

Given that I have never so much as exposed my arms in public, and that until just a few minutes ago I had been concealed, cosseted, and cloistered for most of my nineteen years, I should be leaping out of my chair and running for my life.

But I am too stunned to move.

I am behind a dressing screen, in a back room at a nightclub in Paris, a nude thong barely covering the area that only my future husband is ever meant to see. Apart from that, and two small, circular Band-Aid–type things that have been stuck onto my nipples, and which I am later told are called "pasties," I am naked. The other girls around me, all either blond-haired or black-skinned, are smoking cigarettes and sucking from miniature bottles of champagne. A hairstylist has backcombed my long black hair with such ferocity that I fear I will never get the knots out. Someone else has applied dark purple lipstick to my mouth and slathered pale white foundation on my face,

1

making me look like I am in dire need of a blood transfusion.

I am alone in Paris, almost nude, looking like a corpse, surrounded by smoking, drinking sinners.

I am a Muslim girl, culturally more accustomed to a black veiled burka than this wisp of a panty that is lodged in my backside.

If my elders were here, they would surely impose a fatwa on my head. It happened to Salman Rushdie, I remind myself, for a lot less.

Someone tugs a skinny sweater over my head, instructing me to purse my lips to prevent the purple from staining the white knit. Despite the pasties, my nipples poke through the thin fabric. Someone else squeezes me into a pair of pink leather hot pants. Sparkling high-heeled sandals are thrust onto my hurriedly varnished feet. A wooly coat is thrown on me; a poodle that has been dyed pink is shoved under my arm.

On the other side of the screen, I hear loud, throbbing music. I am pushed toward a short hallway, someone barking in my ear, *"Allez! Allez!"* Staring straight ahead, I see only white-bright lights up high, strange faces reflected in the dark.

I teeter toward them. The poodle pees in my hand.

I hear clapping, whistling, and deafening music.

This is my moment.

Chapter One

If there had ever been such a thing as a Miss Muslim contest, all but one of the women in my family would have won it.

My great-grandmother was named Sundari—which means, simply, "beautiful" in Hindi. Her daughter, my grandmother, was blessed with the moniker Abha, which translates even more vividly into "lustrous beauty." One aunt is Gaura—"fair-skinned" and another Sohalia—"moon river"—to describe the luminescence of her face. They were the beauties of their eras, each one sought out by a man who was prominent and powerful enough to win their hearts.

All of them, except my mother.

Had a Miss Muslim contest ever existed, the beauty-pageant baton that would have been passed on from generation to generation would have stopped at her. Which is why when I was born, Parvez, the midwife who had delivered me at our home in the Mumbai suburb of Mahim, went running through the streets of our neighborhood, joyous and jubilant.

"He has listened!" Parvez yelled out to all. "Allah has visited his blessings on the Shah family once more! This child is most divine!"

They decided to name me Tanaya—which means "child of mine"—and the choice of which came as a great surprise to our relatives. After all, most of the women in my family had been graced with names that signified good looks. And here was I, signifying nothing but ownership.

"Evil eye," my grandfather muttered when my aunt Gaura wondered out loud why I couldn't be named something more symbolic. "Yes, she is fair and dimpled and sweet. But we have been cursed before."

My mother, I was told, sobbed and turned her eyes away as I tried to suckle on her breast. But she instead handed me over to Gaura who had borne a son just eleven days earlier, and who would breastfeed me instead of my own mother.

As a young girl, I had no concept of being attractive. When I looked in the mirror, I saw only a girl who had few friends, a strict grandfather, a grandmother I had loved dearly but who had died when I was not quite seven, a mother who seemed sad most of the time, and a father I had never known.

It wasn't until I was thirteen that I began to notice that I looked a little different compared to other girls my age.

I was taller than everyone else in my class; and even without the benefit of braces, regular skin-whitening treatments, or eyebrow threading sessions, none of which my grandfather—my nana—would ever agree to pay for, people always stared at me, men sometimes longingly. Around then, my nana stopped putting his arm around me as we watched TV on the couch or holding my hand when we went out to buy sticky pink candy from the street vendors or helping me brush my hair at night. When I turned thirteen and my breasts started to blossom and hair appeared in the unlikeliest places, I stopped being my nana's little girl.

It was at about this time that the first sign of my hereditary signature began to appear. All the women in my family, with the exception of my mother, were known for their "Shah streak," a swath of silver-gray across the hairline. It looked like the stripe on a raccoon's tail, a brush of moonlight against a dark night sky. It was, singularly, what had defined almost all of my maternal ancestors—a quirk of nature that graced us virtually without exception, leaving only my mother out. On me, it sprouted tentatively initially, then bloomed. When the first strand came, my aunt Gaura kissed me on the cheek, telling me that in our family, it was considered a mother's blessing, and the more it grew, the more munificent the maternal goodwill. Being that as it may, I had hoped, somewhat naively, that with the appearance of the streak my mother might finally love me a little more.

As my Shah streak grew in and my breasts developed and my stature altered, I was, at fifteen, now as tall and slender as my aunts. My grandfather forbade me from using the public bus to go back and forth from school, knowing about the body-grazing and flesh-pinching that most of the women aboard had to submit to. Whenever he could, he would come by auto-rickshaw to drop and fetch me, rarely letting me out of his sight.

"You are a young woman now," he said to me when I was sixteen. "You have nothing else to offer except the face that Allah has blessed you with. Men of poor moral standing will start to think things when they see you. I believe it is time to settle your mind on the only role you have in this world: a pretty and quiet wife and a devoted mother. Remember that, and you will always be happy."

And I had had no reason not to believe him.

Every teenage girl has a turning point, a time when she realizes that she is more than just the sum of the expectations of her. I finally reached that point two days shy of my nineteenth birthday.

My friend Nilu, who always read copies of *Teen Cosmo* that her brother in London would send her and that she would keep hidden beneath her mattress, would often invite me over to flick through the pages of her latest arrival, to laugh as we scratched and sniffed the fragrant folds of paper with their free perfume samples. On that day, we both stared at the cover of the June issue, on which was a photo of a strikingly skinny girl with long brown hair that seemed to have been partly painted gold. A wind from somewhere blew open her white shirt, revealing a bright pink bra, a tiny diamond sparkling in her belly button. She had her thumbs in her jeans pockets, a glossy pout on her lips, eyes painted silvery purple. She was beautiful, and, from what Nilu and I read of her inside the pages, she was rich and famous, too—a young actress in Hollywood, the words on the page calling her "the next Julia Roberts."

"Why? Where did the old one go?" Nilu asked, looking up at me as I shrugged.

"You know, Tanaya, you are as pretty as this girl," Nilu said, sitting up on her bed and crossing her legs. "In fact, prettier I think. There is nothing she has that you don't— except maybe a jewel in your stomach." She laughed and pushed her glasses, which were sliding down her nose, back up to her eyes. "I don't see why you can't do this," she said, pointing to the pouting girl again.

"Stop being silly, Nilu," I said, getting off the bed.

I finished the last of my cola and headed home. But from that day on, I will have to admit, I started looking at myself in the mirror quite differently: as an image of my aunts and all the other attractive women in my family who had gone before me.

Even when I started to realize my own beauty, I never saw my mother as anything less than perfect. She was forlorn, yes, but how could she not be, with a husband who had left her two months after their wedding and seven months before I was born? For most of my childhood, she had been placid, as if nothing vibrant or wild had ever lived behind those deadened eyes, as if in taking away his love, the father I had never known also took away my mother's very life. It seemed that nothing ever aroused her, excited her, or even saddened her. She was a nebulous character, always in the background of my life, serving no greater purpose than making sure that I ate what was on my plate and that I read the books I brought home from school.

She was this way for every night of my childhood except for one. It had been a grim and rainy day at the height of monsoon season in hot and humid July, and the afternoon had been given over to magazines and television and napping. She was agitated, displaying more emotion than usual, but none of it any use to a bored eight-year-old. At nine o'clock at night, she told me to put on my pajamas and get into bed. I changed into a blue velour pair with a white eyelet lace collar. I lay next to my mother on the bed I shared with her and proceeded to continue reading an Indian comic book—an illustrated tale about a magic monkey that lived in the mountains. She asked me again and again to turn off the light and go to sleep, and again and again I told her that I had just a few more pages to get through. Then, without warning, she reached over to my side of the bed, swiped up the comic book, and flung it across the room onto the speckled pink tile floor. I looked over at her astonished and scared, and saw her hand, its fingers short and thick, coming straight for my face. I felt the sting of the slap, the blood rushing to my right cheek, shocked at the biting sensation in my face. Then she ordered me not to cry, then slapped me again, on the other side. The more I cried and begged her to stop, the more she hit me, until I was crouching in a corner, staring at the black flecks on the rose-colored tiles, my head in my hands. She towered above me, hitting me on both arms, bombarding me with slow punches for what seemed like an eternity. And then, as suddenly as she had started, she stopped, stepping back, wisps of frizzy hair loosened from her braid, her face flush, her mouth agape. She stared for a minute at her two hands, back and front. Then she bent down till she was at my level and put her hand to my cheek again, but this time to stroke it gently.

"Nahin rohna," she said, asking me not to cry. *"Mujhe maaf karo."* She was asking me for forgiveness. I reached over and collapsed on her arm, my drool from crying spilling out onto her printed polyester top. I was suddenly unsure about whether I knew who this woman was. She led me to bed then, laying me down onto starched cotton sheets, her hand on the top of my head. We both lay in the dark, not a sound in the room except for the whirring of a fan standing in the corner. But somewhere in my sobbing and shuddering body, I knew that her accumulated fury at a lost and wasted life was, if nothing else, finally spent.

By the next morning, it was all forgotten—and never mentioned again. After that, I continued, as I had always done, to pay no heed to the hecklers who teased her about her pockmarked skin and pudgy features, instead always rising to defend her. She had been born with a small dark mark that stretched across her right eyebrow, which family superstition had put down to the fact that my grandmother had gazed too long at a funeral procession when she was carrying my mother, and that the sight of so much woe and suffering had shocked the pregnant woman to such an extent that her unborn daughter ended up paying the price for it. I was certain none of this was true—that my mother's "black thing," as everyone called it, was nothing but a birthmark, and that it made her unique. Where I come from, people could be cruel about such things— about the size of one's waist or the closeness of one's eyes. They routinely made up names to describe the neighbors and friends who perhaps had not been blessed by Allah with loveliness. The hefty woman next door was *haathi*— "elephant"—and the local electrician *bakri*—"goat," because of his prominent jaw and the whiskers he chose to adorn it with.

When long-lost relatives from America came to visit one summer when I was nine, looking down at me and then at my mother, the uncle chuckled, saying: "No resemblance. Are you sure you didn't find her somewhere and just bring her home?" He laughed.

My mother went into our room and shut the door. Later, after the uncle had left and my mother emerged once again, she told me that every night for the first five years of her life, my grandmother would massage her nose with a pinch of oil to shape it better. When she was six months old, her chubby little body was waxed. Every day, they slathered a paste made from chickpea flour and lemon on her face to bring out the whiteness they were convinced lay hidden somewhere in her genes.

"All this they did, and for what?" my mother said that evening, still smarting from the hurt of the relative's remarks. "My own husband left me. But you see, my beautiful *beti*, none of this will happen to you. Because of how you look, you will have everything I never did—a man who will stay with you, and a big and boisterous family. If I have given you nothing else in your life, at least I have given you that."

But in truth, a decade later, it was actually Audrey Hepburn who gave me my life.

I had ventured down to Book Nook one day, a book-cum-video library on the street adjacent to ours, and I had decided to rent *Sabrina*, mesmerized by the pixielike black-and-white face on the front of the video box.

I had certainly gotten my pocket money's worth, having watched the movie seven times in six days. Unlike Sabrina, I had no fantasies about the blond beauty of David Larrabee, nor the fantastic wealth of his family. Instead, I was entranced by just one scene in the entire film, the one where Sabrina is at the end of her two years in Paris and is seated at a desk illuminated by a tasseled lamp, writing a letter to her father.

"I have learned how to live, how to be in the world and of the world, and not just to stand aside and watch," she wrote as I mouthed the words along with her over and over again. The doors behind her were open, and I could imagine a warm wind blowing against her soft white gown. I wanted to watch this part only, and nothing else in the movie, but the Rewind button on the machine would often get stuck, so I had no choice but to start at the beginning. But it was that one scene, the one where Sabrina is perfectly poised and peaceful, that lingered in my mind long after I had to return the tape. I immediately resonated with Sabrina's pre-Paris naiveté, with the simple nature of her life, yet her desire for more. She yearned for love, and while I didn't care about that, I still wanted to become what she had become. To be, as she wrote to her father, *"in the world and of the world."*

I resolved that I must one day go to Paris too.

Chapter Two

Of course, I had nobody to whom to confess this profound and utterly ridiculous new desire, one that surprised even me with its pull. Up until I had met Sabrina, I would have been thrilled just to visit Goa, to rock on a fishing boat there, to sit and smell the salt in the air. So I told no one, and prayed that in some distant future our God would find it in his heart to allow a middle-class Muslim girl with a draped head and no money to become another Sabrina.

But perhaps I should not have been too surprised to have this potent longing to gaze through a window at another life. Having never left Mumbai, my only glimpses into the outside world came through my grandfather, who used to cruise across the continents in his capacity as a pilot for Air India before he retired when I was twelve, living on some small investments. But when he was still flying, I used to thrill to the sound of the mailman's footsteps down our corridor, hoping that he would drop into our mailbox another postcard from Nana—this time from

Frankfurt or Singapore or Zurich. I would stare at the pictures on the front of towering pine trees or a perfectly still lake and wonder if I would ever in my life have the grace and good fortune to see such things. And when Nana himself would return, entering through our narrow doorway carrying a small suitcase and with his captain's hat still atop his head, I would rush to him, wanting to throw my arms around his waist. But Nana would only pat me on the head, maybe pinch me lightly on my cheek, before nodding in my mother's direction and retiring to his room. He never talked to me about where he had been and what he had seen. It was only much later that it occurred to me that his reasons for withholding such delectable nuggets of information was to avoid precisely what had happened anyway—that I would be moved to consider life beyond what I knew. All he wanted was for me to become a wife.

So he was overjoyed when, one day, an old classmate approached him with an idea that perhaps his own grandson, one Tariq Khan, would be a good match.

"The boy is educated. A lawyer, living overseas," Nana informed me, squinting through his glasses at the small handwritten words in the letter. "He can come here to view you; that is no problem. He has means."

"But Nana, I am only nineteen. I think I'm too young," I started to protest politely. "I have just finished my studies. Please, allow me to wait for a while."

"Nothing doing," Nana said. "I will write back to my friend today and tell him to have his grandson fly here from London as soon as possible. Time is of the essence, as the boy needs to settle in marriage as soon as he starts his new job. He will be moving soon, in the next few weeks," Nana said, removing his glasses, "to Paris."

I stopped breathing for a second, hearing only the loud thumping of my heart, which at that moment seemed to drown out the other sounds in the room: the radio reciting the news headlines and my mother clanging among pots and pans in the kitchen.

If this was not an act of Allah intervening, I could certainly never find another.

I shook my head at Nana, the first time I had ever done such a thing.

"If you want me to marry him, I will have to go there to meet him, to see if I like the place," I said, my hands sweating. "It will be my new home, after all."

The veins in Nana's temples started to pulsate through his thinning skin, and I could almost see a stream of angry air whistling through his nostrils. My mother, as usual, remained quiet.

"You are a stupid child to even suggest such a thing," Nana said. "You have no passport, no visa, nothing. You cannot go alone, and I will not come with you. Talk sense."

"If he comes here, I will not meet him, and you cannot force me," I said, getting up to go to the bedroom, trembling, stunned at my resolve.

My grandfather stood up, empty peanut shells tumbling from his white kurta onto the floor. He raised his hand above his head as if to slap me on the cheek, but then stopped in midair and lowered his arm.

"I will put this down to the idiocy of youth," he said. "I am running this house and this family. This boy is coming here, and you will marry him."

"I will not," I said, my head spinning. "I will lock myself in the bedroom if I have to. I am certain he is too educated not to be put off by that, and he will then run far away from this family."

Nana, to whom I was almost a daughter, stopped talking to me that day. He stopped asking me about my friends, what activities I had been engaged in, or whether I was close to completing the scarf I had promised to crochet him in time for winter. For the next few days, he just pretended I wasn't there.

Three more letters followed from my grandfather's friend in three weeks, repeatedly asking him to make a decision about Tariq. Each time, my grandfather stared at me in silence, folded the letters, and put them inside the frayed gold-edged pages of the 1972 leather-bound diary that he still carried around proudly, despite it being more than thirty years out of date.

After the fourth and last letter, my grandfather knew there would be no more, as the relatives of male suitors are proud people. He took off his glasses and rubbed his eyes, then called his old boss at Air India from whom he obtained contact names at the local passport office, and then for someone at the Consulate General of France.

His next call was made from outside the house, at one of the long-distance calling booths that occupy virtually every street corner in India, and to which he gruffly asked me to accompany him. He took along his 1972 diary, in the back of which were names of people I'd never heard of, their numbers scratched out and etched in again a dozen times as they, unlike us, moved around. As he waited his turn for the phone, his finger ran down the list, until it settled on REZA AND MINA HUSAIN, a string of long numbers following it.

"Mina-*behen!*" he yelled into the phone, addressing her as a sister. He spoke initially in Hindi and very quickly, aware of the six-second cost increments. Then, almost to ensure that nobody else around him could understand, he started speaking in clipped, proper English.

"That is Tanaya's only condition," he said. "She wants to come to Paris to see the boy. The marriage will definitely take place, but she is being most stubborn." He paused for a second, his heavy brows crinkling beneath his graying hair. "As you know, young people today are different from our day. They don't respect their elders." He shot me a stern glance before turning his attention back to the conversation.

"Thank you, Mina-*behen,*" he said finally. "We have not been in touch for a long time, but we are family after all."

Putting down the receiver, Nana clasped his hand around my arm to lead me out of the booth. His face inanimate and voice cold, he said, "She can't wait to see you."

"But who is she, Nana?" I asked timorously as we walked the short distance back to our apartment. I should have been whooping with delight that my grandfather was making all the arrangements for me to visit a place that had, until that day, been an inconceivable fantasy. "How come I have never heard of her before?"

Mina's grandfather and Nana's late wife had been stepbrother and -sister, born to different mothers. After Nana had moved his family to Mumbai from Pakistan, he and his wife had lost contact with most of the other family members, many of whom had stayed in Lahore. There had been the occasional letter to share some news of celebration or tragedy, but once my grandmother had passed away and her own siblings had begun to die off, the web that had once conjoined the family had slowly disintegrated.

But Nana, being a man of the world, comparatively speaking, chose to do his bit to keep up relations by always having their phone numbers listed in his favorite old diary, even if he did not speak to or see some of these relatives for years at a time.

"She is a widow, and deserves all the respect accorded to one," he said, marching at a brisk pace, his hand still around my upper arm.

"She has lived in Paris for many years, but is Muslim at heart. She has agreed to allow you to stay with her while you indulge this madness of yours. But," he said, turning to me again as we entered our home, "make no mistake,

Tanaya. In our day, we did not have the luxury of meeting our spouses before the wedding. I am only permitting this because I have already agreed to the marriage. Do you understand?"

Nana's frown lines were suddenly deep and dark, reminding me of grooves in a muddy road. Then, with the slight force of his hand on my back, he pushed me into our apartment and slammed shut the door behind us.

Chapter Three

Compared to Mumbai's dry, dusty heat, the Paris air felt chilly on my face.

I stood outside the terminal, clutching a small purse into which I had stuffed one hundred euros and change, converted from Indian rupees. It was a small fortune for my grandfather, and he had given it to me grudgingly, but even though he didn't want me to come to Paris, he certainly didn't want me to starve here.

I had known there would be nobody at the airport to greet me, so Nilu had figured out that the best and cheapest way for me to get from Charles de Gaulle Airport to my aunt's house was on the airport bus.

As I waited for it to appear, with exact change in my hand for the ticket, I stared at a loose leaf of paper that was dancing in the wind, pirouetting on the pavement. I knew there was so much else to see if I would only look up, straight ahead of me. But it was precisely because there was so much to see that I couldn't. I was overwhelmed.

I had never before been among so many foreigners, alone in a strange place. Now that I was finally here, even I was beginning to question my grandfather's decision to send me. It was mid-morning and glorious, and I was surrounded by people. Yet I was as scared as if I were in a dark alley alone at night.

The back of the bus was empty, so I pulled my small trolley bag and brown suitcase down the aisle, shielding my face as I went with my scarf. There I pressed my face against the glass window pane. Some Asian tourists in front of me already had their cameras out, clicking shots of the skyline with its succession of planes taking off and landing. I realized then that I had completely forgotten to bring a camera, and nobody at home had thought to remind me. I was certain that if I had suggested it, my grandfather would have pointed out sternly that I was "not on some jolly vacation."

I smiled as I thought of him, then remembered my coat pocket. I fished inside it and found the piece of paper that he had shoved into my hand just as I was about to board the plane. On it, written very clearly in Nana's dark-blue fountain-pen ink, were Tariq Khan's phone numbers at work and at home. Nana had instructed me to call Tariq as soon as I arrived in Paris, aware that Tariq wouldn't call me, as that was against protocol. His grandfather had made the first overture to mine, and it was for us—as the family of the supposed bride—to make every effort from then on.

But I didn't want to think about any of that. I wanted instead to keep staring out of the window, anxious for the driver to start his engine, impatient to begin the journey that I had only dreamed about.

More than an hour passed before we arrived on the street where my aunt lived, and I followed the directions she had conveyed to my grandfather and found myself standing in front of a low building that stood behind an old, dry, stone fountain. There was a tiny elevator into which I just about managed to squeeze myself and my luggage, the smell of which, oddly, reminded me of home. My aunt's apartment was only one of three that were crowded onto a narrow floor, suddenly dashing my visions of grand halls and curved, polished wooden staircases.

I knocked lightly, and I heard a slow shuffling inside. The door opened, and there she was, the aunt I had never known, dressed in a thick sweater shrugged over a *salwar kameez*, beige-colored socks on her shoeless feet. She looked as if she had just woken up, her hair uncombed, her face weary. Beneath it all though, if I stared hard enough, I could see that she too was probably once very beautiful.

"Hah, you have come," she said, stepping aside to let me in. I reached over to hug her, but instead she forced a smile, patted my back, and turned around.

"Your room is there," she said, pointing to a door halfway down a hallway. "I'm making lunch. Come and eat."

After a meal of lentils and rice, during which Aunt Mina asked me a few cursory questions about my grandfather, I requested her permission to take a shower.

"OK, but quick one," she said. "Water bill comes very high."

Despite my new exotic environment, I dressed the way I always did in India, in a *salwar kameez*, this time with a mismatched shawl covering my head. I pulled a few euros out of my purse and went out, finding a bench at the end of Aunt Mina's street. I sat there for two hours, gazing at the foreign-looking people as they rushed by, on their way to somewhere important, newspapers folded under their arms, a cigarette between long fingers. Then I walked around the block, careful to note the little landmarks I was passing, scared that I might get lost. When I grew familiar with that one street, I walked onto another, then another. I stayed out for five hours, even after I grew hungry and thirsty from all the walking and gawking. But I did not have the courage to enter a store and buy a bottle of water, not knowing how to ask for what I needed, and worried about every euro I would have to spend.

For the next three days, that was all I did. Each day, I went a little farther, marveling at the pretty lace things I would see in a shop window or smelling freshly baked breads outside a bakery, trying to catch even one isolated word from the blurred conversations around me. Three days after arriving, I finally found the courage to walk into a store and buy a bottle of orange juice, drinking in the pulpy sweetness as a silent, solitary toast.

That night, when I returned home, Aunt Mina chastised me for being out of the house.

"Again you are roaming-roaming," she said, not looking up at me from the television, on which a videotape of a Hindi soap opera was playing. "You have come here for a reason, and I'm not understanding why you are spending all your days and money just roaming."

I opened my mouth to say something, but stopped.

"I am not well," she continued, this time turning to look at me. "May Allah help me. Doctor says bad blood pressure, maybe clot is coming. Heart attack. Stroke even. Shazia is arriving tomorrow to care for me. I will need the spare room for my daughter. You can sleep on couch in the meantime, but please, now, you just finish your matter and go back home."

It was evident that she had no interest in hearing from me, so I went into the little bedroom and shut the door. I knew that my mother and Nana, my two closest living relatives, were waiting to hear from me, sitting by the phone in our fluorescent-lit living room. A sense of guilt crept in as I took comfort in the fact that they were unable to contact me unless they left the house and headed to the corner booth, and that the reason for their silence so far had been the expense of such a call—especially so soon after the one initially made to Aunt Mina. I remembered the look on Nana's face as he had said good-bye to me in Mumbai, the tears he would not allow to fall from his eyes, the kiss he gave me on my forehead as he whispered in my ear: "May Allah be with you and keep you safe."

I know I should have been ashamed at myself for misleading them like this, promising one outcome only so I could achieve another.

A small radiator hummed quietly as it hugged the wall. In the suddenly warm room I took off my coat, with the piece of paper with Tariq's number now covered in lint and stuck to a foil candy wrapper. I stared for a moment at a photograph that sat atop a chest of drawers—of Aunt Mina and her daughter, Shazia, for whom I would have to vacate this room the next day. My grandfather had told me a little about Shazia's allegedly wild lifestyle as a single working girl in Los Angeles, referring to her as "a bad sort" and insisting that I not "get any ideas" from her.

The next day, we were back at Charles de Gaulle. My second visit to this airport in only four days was enough to make me feel like a proud veteran of the city. Shazia's plane had been delayed, so as Aunt Mina rested on a low leather seat at the back of the cavernous hall, I walked up and down the arrivals area, occasionally stopping to gaze overhead at the huge board that announced the movements of the planes—where they were going, which ones had just touched down. I watched as well-dressed women in trim pantsuits and high-heeled boots pressed lips with their arriving lovers, and I watched young children throwing their arms around their mothers, who were returning alone from God-knows-where. I wanted to go up to each of these people, to ask them who they were, where they had just been, what they had done there. But of course I did no such thing, not just because I had been trained not to speak to strangers unless absolutely necessary, but also because the only word I had learned in four days was *"bonjour,"* and that wouldn't take me very far.

I noticed then that people were looking at me, too. A group of curly-haired Algerian men clustered around a pay phone whistled as I walked by, one of them raising his eyebrows as if asking me a secret question. I covered my head again with my *dupatta* and hurried past. I walked farther down and leaned for a minute against the railing, my back turned toward the throngs of people arriving. In front of me, two elderly women were seated, and they smiled at me when my eyes caught theirs. One turned to the other and said something quickly in French, and I knew they were talking about me.

"They're saying you're hot," said a voice behind me. I turned around. Shazia was shorter than she looked in the photograph in her room, her face plumper.

"Mummy said you would be here. I knew it was you, even from the back," she said, giving me a hug, still on the other side of the metal railing as a security guard hurried her along. "I was thinking, who else would be covered head-to-toe on a beautiful night like this? Wow," she said, her eyes resting on the silver streak in my hair. "I'd heard about that, but thought people were making it up. Can I touch?"

26

I smiled and hugged her again after she had made her way to my side of the railing, the side on which she now belonged. Despite the length of her journey, she smelled like fresh lemons. I liked her immediately.

"Where's Mummy?" she asked, pulling off her sweater and wrapping its sleeves around her waist.

"Over there, sitting down. She's not feeling so well," I said.

"Come," Shazia said, leading me by the hand. "Let's go get her and head home."

The Metro was full, but a man gave up his seat for Aunt Mina while Shazia and I held on to the plastic straps that hung from the ceiling, holding between us a pile of bags and jackets and shawls.

"You never know what the weather will be like here," Shazia said, motioning to all her stuff. "In Paris, you have to be prepared.

"So have you been enjoying your stay here? Mummy said you came here to see a boy." For the last part of that sentence, Shazia slid into a Pakistani accent. She wobbled her head from side to side, uttering the words just as her mother might—or mine for that matter—and then giggled at her own insolence.

"Yes, I came to see a boy, but haven't seen him yet," I said, wanting to change the subject quickly. "How was your flight? Long way from Los Angeles, yes?"

"Not as long as coming from India," she said. "You really must have wanted to be here."

"Yes," I replied, my eyes now turned downward as I thought guiltily of how I was avoiding phoning home. "It was my dream to come." Shazia smiled at me and reached up to pull away a few strands of my hair that had become affixed to my lip gloss.

"Well, I'm glad you're here," she said. "I've come to look after Mummy for a while, but not 24/7, so we can hang out together, paint the town red and all that."

I wasn't sure what she was talking about, but I certainly liked the sound of it.

The following evening, Shazia and I took a taxi—the first time I had been in one since arriving in Paris—and went to the Buddha Bar, which she told me was one of the most fashionable places in all of Paris. We entered into a space that was as dark as it was loud, handed our coats to a girl sitting in a small cubicle, and almost collided with a waitress in a red-and-gold silk dress carrying a tray of multicolored drinks. Shazia grabbed my wrist and took me down a flight of stairs. I stopped in the middle of the restaurant and stared up at an enormous golden Buddha that dominated the room.

"You can close your mouth now," Shazia said, smiling. "You're wowed. We get it." She pulled me over to a long table at the back that was filled with her friends. She hugged and kissed all of them and introduced me as her cousin from Mumbai. They all nodded enthusiastically, some of them recounting a trip to Rajasthan or Calcutta or how their boss/roommate's boyfriend/neighbor is from

India, as if that would help me feel more welcome. I sat next to Shazia and a girl she used to work with, unable to pay any attention to their conversation. I couldn't take my eyes off the Buddha; the girls in their short, sharp dresses and high shoes; or the men in their smart shirts tucked into jeans. Everyone had a cigarette in one hand and a drink in the other, dancing in their own world to music that boomed through the speakers. My eyes began to smart with all the smoke, and nobody else said a word to me the whole night, but there was nowhere else I wanted to be.

I realized then that Paris with a friend—or better, a far-removed cousin who had become a friend—was a lot less lonely than it had been. Shazia had lived here most of her life, so knew the city as intimately as anyone would. Every day, Aunt Mina would ask me when I was leaving, if I had "finished my matter," but Shazia would take me by the hand and, ensuring that her mother was tended to for the next couple of hours, would tell her to "stop bugging" me and would take me out.

In the few days after Shazia arrived, once she had recovered from the jet lag, she showed me the Paris that only insiders know. She had said we would do all the tourist things, like window-shop around Saint-Germain, go boating down the Seine, take coffee and croissants at Les Deux Magots, and ride the elevator to the top of the Eiffel Tower.

But we also visited her friends who lived in a basement apartment that had been transformed into something that reminded me of pictures in an old storybook of Aladdin's Cave, and others who took us out for Chinese food in a restaurant that was an hour's Metro ride from our home, but worth it for the fragrance of the rice and the crispiness of the steamed vegetables. On a sunny afternoon, we went to the Île St-Louis and ate the creamiest ice cream I had ever tasted in my life, its flavor lingering on my tongue long after I'd finished the last spoonful. French words came tumbling out of her mouth at every turn, and I made it a point to learn what I could from her, loving to imitate her irritated *"mais non!"* and enthusiastic *"bah oui!"* and the string of *"alors"* that referred to nothing in particular.

"You'll get there," she said smiling. "It's actually an easy language to learn, once you get the hang of it."

"You say that as if I'll be here forever," I said as we stood one evening on the Pont Neuf, watching the lights of the city flicker in the distance. "I came here to do something, and I've not done it yet." The guilt resurfaced. The slip of paper still lay in the pocket of my coat.

"It's never easy going against the grain." Shazia's voice was suddenly quiet, the darkness of the river seeming to mirror her momentary mood. "I did it, and I'm still paying the price."

Shazia's father, Reza, a Pakistani immigrant who had opened a small tourist store on the farthest reaches of the rue de Rivoli twenty years ago, had left Lahore to seek out a better life for his wife and their infant daughter, and had ended up first in England, working at an Indian restaurant in Birmingham. When he one day overheard a table of diners talking about a trip they had just made to Paris, and all the wonderful shops they had seen there, something in his heart stirred, and he instantly believed that that was where he could make a good living.

Shazia was five years old when her parents took the ferry from Dover to Calais and headed straight to the French capital. Her father had purchased a secondhand Linguaphone system to learn some basics of the language, but with his heavy Lahore accent—slightly tinged by the broad Birmingham brogue he had acquired—it was not surprising that nobody could understand him.

But still, he was fortunate to find a small space on the heavily traveled tourist street, and put down most of his life savings for the first and last months' rent and a security deposit. With what little he had left, he rented a studio apartment in the Latin Quarter, all three of them living in one room. Shazia told me that her mother cried every day for a month after coming to this country, baffled by the language and the habits and the incessant smoking of these people. But Shazia took to it instantly, picking up the language as if it were her own. After a decade of working hard and saving everything, Reza was able to buy a larger place, with a bedroom for their only daughter who was fast becoming a woman.

Reza died three years ago. He had been stabbed in the back by a burglar who had forced his way into the store at closing time, then made off with four hundred francs from the register and a pile of *J'ADORE PARIS* sweatshirts. Reza's blood was splattered over the rest of his stock, dripping from the small shot glasses embellished with motifs of the Arc de Triomphe and the porcelain platters featuring Moulin Rouge dancers.

"Gypsies," the police had said, as Aunt Mina lay crumpled in a heap on the floor, Shazia holding on to her but feeling desperately faint herself. "They used to be just petty thieves. But now, they find knives."

Shazia, who had been working as a legal secretary in an American law practice at the time, for a short while thought about quitting her job and taking over her father's small shop, to honor the man he had become and the decent business he had built on his own.

But a week after his murder, she stood alone in the store and stared at the now cleaned-up merchandise and the empty cash register, and knew she would be miserable, consigned forever to her father's death.

"The place is cursed," Aunt Mina had said. "I have already lost him here. I will not sleep another night in my life if you start working here too."

So Shazia went back to work at her shiny office near the Place de la Concorde while her mother stayed home and wept and prayed for Allah to come and take her away too.

There was insurance money, and Shazia was earning well, so they lived comfortably. But Mina had never known anything but marriage, and now the only reason she had come to this country was gone. It was her dream, she kept saying, to return to Lahore to live out her days. Once her daughter was married off, that was what she would do.

"And then I got the transfer," Shazia said, telling me the story that first night. "California. Los Angeles. Sunshine three hundred and sixty-five days of the year. Oh my God, how could I not go?"

Aunt Mina fell into a heap again when her daughter told her she was moving out and leaving home, and neither threats nor begging did anything to convince Shazia otherwise. On the day she was leaving, her mother rammed a *taveez*—a talisman to ward off bad luck—into her daughter's bag, kissed her on the forehead, and pleaded with her to return soon. Shazia sent money every month, along with letters and photographs describing her new Los Angeles life, all of which made Mina yearn for Lahore even more.

"We are the same, you and I," Shazia said to me as we stared over the bridge into the Seine. "We are the only children in our families, only daughters, both fatherless, both with mothers too consumed in their own grief to really look at us." Shazia wiped away a tear, the first time I had seen her show any emotion.

"We are like sisters," she said, linking her arm in mine. "And I will do everything I can to help a sister."

Chapter Four

My first ten days in Paris passed as if in a dream—watery, surreal, almost too quickly to savor.

On day eleven, a mere seventy-two hours before I was scheduled to return to Mahim, the future I had been avoiding showed up on my doorstep.

In the middle of the afternoon, when Aunt Mina was napping and Shazia was chatting lazily on the phone with one of her old school friends, the doorbell rang. I peered through the peep-hole, and knew instantly who it was.

"Tanaya?" he asked, as I opened the door.

I nodded silently.

"You are even lovelier than I expected," he said, smiling. "It's nice to meet you. I'm Tariq."

He was about to extend his hand, but stopped upon realizing that it was perhaps too Western a gesture for me to embrace. I quickly covered my head and stepped aside so he could come in. We stood in the narrow doorway, me too uncomfortable to suggest he approach any farther, him picking up on that.

"I never heard from you," he said. "I wanted to make sure that you were OK, that nothing had happened to you. I didn't have a phone number, only an address. Through my grandfather. You know how old-fashioned these people are." He smiled and shrugged, his features broad and handsome. In each ear dangled a tiny gold loop, the only things about him reminiscent of a glorious Mughal heritage and accoutrements that looked strangely complementary to his dark suit and tie.

"I'm sorry I didn't call. I'm fine," I said, nervously fingering one end of my *dupatta*. I hadn't thought through what I was going to tell my family when I returned home. My grandfather had finally called a few days before, but I was out, as usual, with Shazia. Aunt Mina had answered the phone, but told me later that she informed my grandfather that she had "no idea" about any alliance between Tariq and me.

"I don't know where you have been going," she had said to me later. "You deal with this yourself with your Nana. I do not wish to get involved." Nana had told Aunt Mina to instruct me to call him back. I hadn't done so yet.

"I'm not going to ask you why you didn't contact me," said Tariq. "We all have our own reasons for doing things. I thought it was weird myself, a girl flying all the way from India to view me. It's unusual, you know. But I wanted to be open-minded. Living away from Pakistan has altered my outlook."

For a second, I remembered Sabrina, the girl who had led me here. I closed my eyes for a moment and wanted to recall what I had been seeking, what had brought me here. I still wasn't "of the world." I was still standing on the side-lines and watching. Perhaps it took longer than two weeks. After almost a fortnight here, I was still the same girl. I re-mained silent, my eyes on the floor, knowing that I had no explanation.

"Well, I may as well get going," he said. "As long as nothing happened to you." He turned to face the door, then turned around again.

"Don't worry about anything," he said. "I will take care of it."

When Shazia got off the phone, I told her about my unex-pected visitor. She laughed gleefully and then raised her hand, expecting me to slap it, an odd mannerism that she had displayed numerous times.

"Well, at least *that's* over with," she laughed. "He got the message. You're done with him."

"You don't understand," I said to her quietly, keeping my voice down so Aunt Mina wouldn't overhear. "They only sent me here on the express condition that I would agree to marry him. I didn't even call him. What will I tell them when I go home?"

"What makes you think you're going home?" she asked.

❀   ❀   ❀

When the phone rang the next day, I knew instinctively that it was Nana. I decided to answer it myself.

"Tanaya? *Beti!* Where have you been?" he asked. I could imagine him frowning, his face red, and I could hear the chatter of voices in the background, other people crammed into booths next to his.

"Sorry, Nana, that I've not called. I've been meaning to, but with the time difference and all," I said lamely. "Everything is OK. I am OK."

"Everything is *not* OK!" he shouted. "I have just had a call from Tariq's grandfather. I understand that the boy has rejected you. I am ashamed. What did you do wrong?"

My mind went blank for a second, before I realized that that was what Tariq meant when he said he would take care of things. It was far more acceptable for him to turn me down than for me to have never even called him in the first place.

"I did nothing, Nana. I met him. I was pleasant."

"Did you do something to your face? He was told you were a beauty. Did you change something? Do you have a pimple?"

"No, Nana, nothing," I said, embarrassed. "Maybe he just didn't like me."

"Hah!" he grunted. "So much expense to send you there, and for what? I told my friend that I will never speak to him again, that his grandson is ill-mannered and unworthy of our efforts. How dare he turn down a Shah girl!"

37

"Sorry to disappoint you, Nana. But it is all the will of Allah," I said, trying to appease him.

He told me he had made arrangements to pick me up from the airport in Mumbai three days hence, and I quickly hung up.

The next morning, Paris was in its fullest glory. Shazia and I had decided to take a walk down the Champs-Elysées, and I marveled once again at its wide tree-lined streets and the sparkling stores that dotted our path. The sun was high in a pale blue sky, and a calm wind rustled my polyester-chiffon ensemble and caused a slight chill to cover my bare feet. I couldn't imagine that in forty-eight hours, into which I was planning to cram a lot, I would be back at my home in Mahim, with nothing but the incessant rumbling of the trains from the railway station across the street to keep me company. The building we lived in was called Ram Mahal—literally "God's Palace"—so named because when my grandfather had first bought our apartment there decades ago it was indeed a palace relative to the other buildings in the area. It had originally been painted a light yellow, but after forty years of monsoon rains and no upkeep, the exterior was now chipped and gray, with none of the pleasant prettiness of its heyday. Each of the five floors boasted a small courtyard, in which the children of the building would play catch and hide-and-seek, drinking tongue-pinching Limca from dirty glass bottles. There was no elevator, so the oldest and most infirm of the building's residents remained at home for years on end, having everything brought to their door, finally having to be carried out on a stretcher. As a child, I used to love running up and down the stone steps, lit only by a single hanging bulb, feeling the smooth, thick curves of concrete banisters as I went from floor to floor visiting my friends. It had been the only building in the neighborhood to offer indoor plumbing. But now merely turning off the side street and into the entrance would yield the overpowering stench of human waste. In the last twenty years or so, squatters had set up camp right across the street, living beneath tents made from bamboo sticks, blue plastic sheets, and coarse burlap rice sacks. Small children, their hair crawling with lice, their clothes tattered but their tiny eyes still lined with *kohl*, would stand on the street and beg for a few rupees from the occupant of a passing car, or else they would forage for leftovers in the big mounds of trash that often lay uncollected in the street for weeks at a time.

"I really don't want to go back there," I said suddenly, shaking my head, turning to Shazia, as we continued our walk down the thoroughfare.

"Then don't," she replied, stopping. She put her hand on my arm. "Tanaya, you'll think I'm crazy, but I honestly feel like you belong here. Like Paris isn't done with you. I don't think you should go home now."

The wind felt cooler, and I wrapped my sweater tightly around me.

"But I have to go. There's no way I can stay here. My ticket is 'non-refundable-non-rerouteable-non-endorsable,'" I said, repeating my grandfather's stern directive. "If I don't use the return portion, it will go to waste."

"That's what return tickets from Paris are for. Wasting," she said. "Look, come and sit a minute." She led me to a nearby bench, and we eased ourselves down. I ran my finger over a rusty nail that held the painted green planks in place, confused about the conversation that Shazia and I were starting to have.

"I've been in your shoes," she said. "I wanted to be somewhere else and it upset everyone. But I did it, because I had to. I know it's hard. But see how long it took you to get out. What are you going back to Tanaya? Tell me."

"My family," I said softly. "My usual life. That's all."

"Please," she said, rolling her eyes. "From what you've told me, you don't have much going on there. I mean, it's hardly like anyone is lining up to make a reality show on you."

I blinked, not really knowing what Shazia was talking about, but understanding her point anyway. I knew that since things hadn't worked out with Tariq, Nana would enroll me in the nearby Mrs. Mehra's Institute of Domestics. All the girls in my neighborhood went there if marriage was for any reason delayed, and six months later "graduated" with important knowledge such as how to pickle lemons, how to remove stains from limestone, and

how to best iron a man's shirt so that the collar lies flat just
so. I had assumed that I would go there too. I told Shazia
this now, and she let out one of her typical guffaws.

"It's like your whole life has been missing," she said.
"Mrs. Mehra is going to have to wait."

The thud resonated in my ear long after I had put the
receiver down. Fear—terror, actually—had helped keep
my voice steady for the past fifteen minutes, but once Nana
had ended the call, and no doubt dispensed with his love
for me at the same moment, I allowed myself to sob on
Shazia's shoulder.

She had stood next to me as I had spoken to him, her
hand on my back, nodding sympathetically as if she were a
nurse and I were a patient trying to down some foul-
tasting medicine. She held my hand as I told Nana that I
wasn't planning to use the return portion of the ticket he
had purchased for me, even after he reminded me that it
was nonrefundable, as if that were the only thing that mattered. I told him that I didn't want to return to Mahim just
yet because there was nothing there for me. I know his
heart must have withered a little at hearing this, because if
there was nothing else in Mahim, at least there was him. I
told him that soon enough I would go home, just not now.
I was about to use Shazia as an example, but then thought
the better of it. Nana presciently asked me, however,
"Does that godforsaken girl have anything to do with

this?" For a moment, his voice had sounded controlled. But when he realized that I wasn't just teasing or testing him, that I was going to remain in Paris indefinitely, more or less on my own, he shouted at me with such wild anger that I was certain all our neighbors had heard him, as well as the slum-dwellers across the street. He called me names that I had never heard uttered by him: "whore" and "mad cow" and "bloody stupid ungrateful bitch." I heard my mother yelling something in the background, but Nana was ignoring her as he always did, and despite my protestations that I would be OK, that I would manage somehow, Nana placed a curse on my head. In a voice dark with fury, sore with unshed tears, he said that Allah would punish me for my sins, that I would be maimed or paralyzed or left to die in a gutter.

"You want to live alone?" he shouted. "Go on, live alone. Let somebody come in the middle of the night and rape and murder you. You deserve it." Then, his voice quiet again, he said, "And if Allah spares you, never come home to us. You are already dead to me."

Then came the thud. My mother never even came on the phone. I thought of the last time I had seen them, at the airport as they were bidding me farewell, my grandfather expectant that I would return an engaged woman, my mother expressionless on the sidelines. I remember thanking them both for letting me go.

I looked at Shazia, and she hugged me.

"I'm making a horrible mistake," I said then, through tears. "I should never have let you talk me into this. It seemed like a joke, but it's not." Suddenly I was angry with her. "They trusted me, and I abused it. You may feel like it's OK to live without family. I do not. They are all I have. I'm changing my mind. I'm going home today as planned. I must call them back now," I said, panic filling my voice as I picked up the phone again.

She grabbed my upper arm forcefully, pulling me back toward her.

"As hard as it seems now, you *are* doing the right thing," she said. "It's not your fault that your family is so intolerant. You're almost twenty, a young woman. What—they expect you to get married and have children of your own, while still treating *you* as a child? Your grandfather was just angry. He will recover, and they will accept you back when you are ready. But now your life is here. I can see it in your heart, that it's what you really want. Trust me. I'm never wrong about these things."

"But what will I do here?" I asked. "How will I live? Where will I live? Your mother wants me out. Who will give me pocket money?"

"It's OK," Shazia said, lifting my chin up with her fingers and wiping away the tears from my cheeks. "I have it all figured out. And you know what they say—*inshah Allah*—if it is the will of God for you to remain here, then all the pieces will fall into place."

43

We went into the guest room, and she helped me pack my things. She then led me to Aunt Mina, who was resting in her room, so I could say good-bye. Mina assumed I was on my way to the airport, wished me well on my journey, turned over onto her side, and went back to sleep.

Chapter Five

At my new home, Zoe was sitting cross-legged on a blue couch, chewing gum that smelled of spearmint. She reached up to kiss me hello. She had an unusually long neck, short dark hair that hugged a pretty, if rather angular, face. Her eyes were blue and friendly, her skin translucent. A strappy white T-shirt stopped just short of white drawstring pants, and around her right ankle were three gold chains of varying thickness.

Shazia reminded me that I had met Zoe during one of our recent nightlife outings, but we had visited so many places and met so many people that by this point all these white faces were a blur.

"Nice to see you again," Zoe said, removing the gum from her mouth, folding it into a pink tissue and picking up a packet of cigarettes. She offered me one, but I politely shook my head. Shazia, meanwhile, reached out and pulled one out of the pack. I had seen Shazia do a lot of things in these past two weeks, but never smoke, so her ease with lighting up and inhaling took me by surprise.

"Zoe is from the States," Shazia informed me. "But she's been living here a long time. What, like fifteen years or something, right?" Shazia asked her friend.

"Give or take," Zoe drawled, smoke circling out of her mouth. "Came here to study, married a Frenchman, but that was a disaster. Even so, I never left. This place is addictive, you know?" She was staring at me, looking for agreement, so I nodded.

"Your parents didn't mind?" I asked her, finally speaking. "They were OK with you leaving to come here?"

"Hell, I was over eighteen, could do what I pleased," Zoe replied, smirking. I felt ridiculed.

As Shazia and Zoe casually discussed the more recent details of their respective lives, their conversation alternating between French and English, I took advantage of their momentary distraction to look around. It was a cramped but comfortable living room, painted in varying shades of blue, cream, and white. On a far wall was a large framed print—swirls of orange on a bright yellow background—that was so vivid compared to the relatively calm colors of the rest of the room, I felt dizzy for a moment. A dining table was stacked with newspapers and unopened mail; a couple of armchairs, creased and crumpled, looked as if they had been happily occupied over the years. A blanket lay on the floor close to a small fireplace, and a stained coffee mug sat on another table. The phone was taken off its hook, and jazz music was playing softly from a radio. It was a deeply comforting environment, but even so, I felt awkward and out of place.

I had no idea what we were doing here.

"It would just be for a while," Shazia said as I turned my attention back to them. "Until we figure something else out."

"Shaz, anything for you," Zoe said, smiling and putting out her cigarette, much to my relief. The smoke in the small room was beginning to cause my eyes to dry out. "She can sleep here; this couch folds out into a pretty decent bed."

They spoke of me as if I wasn't even there, and while I was used to that happening in Mahim, I had thought that Shazia would treat me differently.

"I need to use the restroom," Zoe said, lifting her long, lean frame from the couch.

"What's this?" I whispered to Shazia when we were alone. "You're leaving me here?"

"I had to take you *somewhere*," Shazia whispered back. "Look, Zoe is really nice. She's a foreigner too, so she completely gets it. I figured you could stay here for a couple of weeks, help out around the house, maybe cook, in exchange for having a roof over your head. By then, I'm sure I'll find you a job and then we'll see where to put you."

At that moment for the first time since the decision was made for me to stay on, I was truly beginning to regret it.

Suddenly I felt untethered, unwanted—a burden to everyone. I had no home, no job, no money. In Mahim, Nana
had given me an allowance every week, which I would
spend on my regular visits to Book Nook, or drinking cold
coffee with Nilu at our favorite neighborhood café. There,
at least, I belonged to someone. Here, now, on this cool
Paris night, my grandfather's curses still searing my ears,
all I wanted to do was go back home.

Chapter Six

Shazia was to spend another two weeks in Paris tending to her mother before heading back to Los Angeles. But after the evening that she dropped me off at Zoe's, I didn't see much of her. She had called a couple of days later, telling me that her mother's health had worsened and that she would be spending more time with her. I wanted to tell her that I didn't like being left alone like this, but based on what she appeared to be going through in her own family travails, thought it selfish to burden her further.

So I spent my first few days as Zoe's flatmate-cum-housekeeper in a subtle state of shock, still numb from being disowned by the only family I had ever known, unable to feel any joy at this so-called freedom I was experiencing. I was still waiting for Allah to smite me at every turn.

Zoe taught English at a nearby school, so was gone for most of the day. As she whizzed out the door every morning, a thermos of coffee in one hand and a paper bag containing a buttery croissant in the other, I cleaned up after her. She had told me that her ex-husband used to call her "Hurricane Zoe," and I could see why. When she was busy, she always seemed to do everything at breakneck speed. That left little time for picking up after herself, so, given the tacit agreement between her and Shazia, I stepped into that role. I washed her pajamas and towels after she had tossed them on the floor, made her bed, cleaned her kitchen. I didn't mind it, as the routine of it was at least something familiar, something that connected me to what my mornings used to be back in Mahim. And it wasn't like I had much else to do. The apartment was so small that I was done cleaning by noon, and then I would turn on the television and listen to the flurry of French words until I came across something I could recognize: *"demain,"* or *"peut-être"* or *"il y a,"* fully cognizant that being able to only say "tomorrow," "maybe," or "there is" would get me almost nowhere in Paris.

I always dreaded Zoe coming home, not for any other reason except that I would have to make some weak-hearted attempt to have a conversation with her. As pleasant as she was to me, I was painfully aware that she was only allowing me to stay here as a favor to an old friend, and I was certain that she often looked at me and wondered when I would leave, returning her living-room couch to her.

"So, like Shazia, you're Muslim too, right?" she asked me one evening as we ate a dinner of pasta and steamed vegetables in front of the television.

"Yes. But not the terrorist kind," I said without really thinking, then realizing how stupid that sounded.

"Oh, I'm sure," she said, startled at my response. "That's not what I meant."

"I know," I replied sheepishly, slurping an oily strand into my mouth. "It's just . . . you know how it is these days. You say 'Muslim,' and everyone imagines long beards and bombs. Most of us are not like that. I don't think I know anyone who would be prepared to strap dynamite on himself."

Although Zoe didn't ask, I told her about the religious diversity of our apartment complex, how our neighbors were Christian, Hindu, Sikh, Parsee, even Jewish.

"What about the killings—religious tension and all that stuff?" she asked. "Don't Hindus and Muslims hate each other?"

"They're not the best of friends, but we try and live peacefully together—not always successfully." I realized I was speaking like an outsider already, like somebody no longer a part of that world. "Nilu, my best friend, is Hindu." I suddenly missed her. By now, I figured, given the speedy manner in which news both significant and trivial was passed down our street, she would have heard about my absconding. Knowing Nilu, though, she would probably have been proud of me.

"I've always wanted to visit that part of the world," Zoe said, setting down her plate and turning to look at me. "But I was a student for the longest time, then got married, then had the baby, and somehow never got around to it. Now that I'm free again though, I should look into it."

Zoe's random admission, that she had had a child, stunned me for a moment—and not just because I could hardly imagine a fetus being housed in that skinny belly or passing through those sinewy hips. There were no indications in the apartment that this woman had ever encountered motherhood—no photographs of a smiling, swaddled child, no crayon sketches pinned to the refrigerator door, not even a stuffed animal lying around.

"She's five now," Zoe said. "Lives with her father. I haven't seen her since she was three months old, and that's fine by me." Her gaze suddenly shifted off my face, moved past my ear, and landed somewhere on the metal window frame behind me. "You know how most mothers say, 'I can't imagine life without my child'? Well, I could. And I did, all the time. I felt no connection to her whatsoever, and didn't want my life to change because she was all of a sudden in it. So when my husband and I split, and he wanted custody of her, I told him he could have it. Best decision I ever made."

She stood up to take the plates into the kitchen while I sat quietly and digested this new information. I wondered, for a minute, if my mother had wanted to give me up too, if she had felt any connection to me when I was born. I wondered if maybe the reason she kept me around was because she had no ex-husband to pass me off to.

"What was her name?" I called out to Zoe, who was still in the kitchen.

"Who?"

"Your daughter. What was her name?"

"Oh," she replied, pausing for a second. "Emily."

It sounded like she had forgotten, as if she hadn't thought of her child since the day she gave her away.

Chapter Seven

My father, Hassan Bhatt, was the youngest of five sons and a member of a prominent family in Lahore. He was tall enough, rich enough, and of decent enough character—all of which seemed to qualify him as the perfect candidate for the job of my mother's husband, a position that many other men were supposedly vying for based on our family's legacy of exceptional beauty in our women.

Only, as was the way things were done back then, Hassan Bhatt never saw my mother until the wedding ceremony was about to begin. He had never thought to assume that she would be anything less than stunning, because no woman in my family ever had been. He admitted later that he might have heard someone comment, as the engagement was being announced, that my mother was "not *quite* as lovely as the other sisters, but not bad." For Hassan Bhatt, "not bad" was good enough, and surely would still be divine. Perhaps he should have been tipped off by my mother's name. Where her sisters were given appellations that spoke of loveliness, my mother had been christened Ayesha — named after the wife of the prophet Muhammad, the founder of Islam. It was a noble name, no doubt. But Hassan Bhatt, as it turned out, was not in the least bit interested in nobility.

Aunt Sohalia told me years later of the look that appeared on Hassan Bhatt's face when the red chiffon bridal scarf that covered my mother's head was first lifted. She described the look as one of "severe disappointment," but nobody said a word, not even the bridegroom. And in my grandfather's mind, there wasn't even an inkling of a notion that this sudden and rather unseemly revelation should be an impediment to my mother's marital happiness, given that, after all, Hassan Bhatt was far too decent a man, and from far too upstanding a family, to abandon a marriage simply because he didn't like the way his wife looked.

For one of the few times in his life, Nana was wrong.

There had been a honeymoon planned, in Ooty, a snow-capped vacation resort in India, but that had been abruptly cancelled when Hassan Bhatt announced that he had some pressing business to take care of in Lahore. Although he tried to convince my mother otherwise, she went with him, assuming that the rest of her life would be spent by his side, being his wife.

Two months later, she was back in Mahim, at her father's house, with me in her belly, no larger than a grain of rice.

Nineteen years later, my mother had yet to recover from the humiliation of being left by a husband because of the way she looked — or didn't. I would catch her occasionally looking at their wedding photograph, a bland black-and-white shot framed in gold that she kept in the bottom drawer of a chest in our bedroom. I had often snuck in there to look at it myself, to gaze at the wide-eyed nervousness on my mother's face and the momentous sadness on that of Hassan Bhatt's, my nana standing cautiously behind them.

Chapter Eight

Soon after Zoe had left for work one morning, just as I was about to wring out the laundry and hang it up to dry in the small, square-shaped bathroom, Shazia arrived. She smiled broadly, as if I had just seen her yesterday, as if I was neither homeless nor penniless nor jobless in a still-strange city.

"How are you doing?" she asked, throwing her arms around me.

"OK," I replied. "How's your mother feeling?"

"Better, actually. I think me being here has really helped. We've been spending lots of time at home these past couple of weeks, just her and I. It's been good. I've promised her I'll come back as soon as a let-up in my work schedule allows it. I'm flying back to L.A. tomorrow.

"What about you?" she asked, finally turning her attention back to me again.

I had started to resent Shazia for encouraging me to do something as foolhardy as this, and it finally began to show.

And now, she was returning to Los Angeles, leaving me behind.

"What am I doing?" I said to her, turning back toward the living room while she slipped off her coat and followed me. "This was a stupid idea, and I should never have allowed you to talk me into it. But I have nobody to blame but myself. I want to go home, but Nana won't take me back, I'm sure of it. Once he says these things, he never changes his mind."

"Oh, stop feeling sorry for yourself," Shazia said, her voice laced with recrimination, her face utterly lacking in sympathy. "You're not a kid anymore. And it's only been a couple of weeks. You'll be fine, honest. You'll be better than fine. We all have problems. I was supposed to marry a boy from Karachi, but he rejected me flat-out. Said I was too fat. I promised myself I would never put myself through that humiliation again."

"I didn't know," I said softly. "You never mentioned."

"Well, it's not something I like to talk about," Shazia said, the bitterness in her face now yielding. "It just made me really resent our culture, you know? There's a lot about it that sucks."

"I'm sorry you feel that way, but I'm still proud of where I come from," I said, aware that I was sounding naïve. "I can't imagine never returning to India."

"Nobody's saying that," she said. "But it's OK to develop an affinity with another land, another culture. It doesn't make you any less Muslim. I'm Muslim, but I'm

American as well. I can't tell you who the Pakistani prime minister is, but I know the name of Kate Hudson's baby." She laughed.

She pulled me down onto the couch and took a sheet of yellow lined paper out of her bag.

"Look, good news," she said. "A job, a permanent place to live, how to get your visa extended . . . Everything you need. You start next week."

I glanced down and saw a scribbled name of a café with an address and phone number. Below that were other addresses, other numbers. My entire new life, according to Shazia, whittled down into a few scrawled lines.

"A good friend of mine owns a cute café, very trendy, in Odéon. He needs a cashier, which I thought would be perfect for you because you don't really have to speak. His English is great, so at least you can communicate. It's a cash job—he pretty much only hires illegals," said Shazia, lowering her voice although we were alone. "The pay isn't bad, and it's enough to share a place I found with a few other girls. Those are the details there," she said, pointing to the second address. "You can walk to work, and all the girls keep strange hours, so you'll have the place to yourself a lot. It's perfect," she said, folding her hands on her lap, a look of smug satisfaction on her face.

"I'm glad *you* think so," I said, the resentment returning. "I don't want any of it. I want to go home."

Shazia's face softened, and she put her hand on top of mine. "Listen, all those dreams you came here with, you still have to achieve them," she said. "You haven't had your Sabrina moment yet, have you?"

I shook my head, disconsolate, but now feeling embarrassed by my delusion.

"You can't leave here until you feel what you said you wanted to feel," Shazia said. "Not until you can show everyone you are no longer just the pretty Shah girl from Mahim."

I nodded, carefully folded up the sheet of paper, and rose to bid my distant cousin a final good-bye.

My brown suitcase sat behind me in the cashier's booth, waiting to be taken to its new home. It still bore half-peeled-off stickers from my grandfather's travels—a dozen or so faded Air India tags dotted over its surface, the familiar yellow-and-red Maharajah now grimy with age.

Another bill was brought to me, a shiny credit card placed upon it, and I swiped it through the small machine on my right, punched in a code, ripped out the resulting printout, and placed it back on the tray for the waiter to return to his customer. I had been doing this for five hours and twenty minutes, off and on, and when it was slow I leafed through the English–French dictionary that Shazia had given me before she left.

The place was called, simply, Café Crème, because it professed to specialize in the sweet creamy drink, although as far as I could tell, so did every other café in the vicinity— or in the rest of Paris, for that matter. The owner's name was Mathias, which took me a while to learn how to pronounce, and he was a good friend of Shazia's, although neither one of them told me how. He was part German, was multilingual and fluent in English, which made my first day more comfortable than I had thought it might be. Like with Zoe, I knew he only had me around as a favor to Shazia, but he didn't seem to mind it. He had a dimple on his left cheek that creased happily when he smiled, a mop of light brown hair, and slender eyes surrounded by long lashes. He seemed to do everything in the café, stepping in to take orders when it was busy, stocking the refrigerator with new supplies, even sweeping the floor at closing time, a pen constantly wedged in his mouth.

He had greeted me one morning with a hug and a kiss on each cheek, which is certainly not the way I imagined new employees would be received at work in India. He had started speaking to me in French, shifting suddenly to English when he saw the look of alarm on my face. He had motioned to my outfit with a wave and had uttered a *"très exotique"* before continuing on with his instructions. My hours were eleven in the morning till seven in the evening, with an hour off for lunch and fifteen-minute breaks every other hour for, as he put it, "a coffee and a cigarette." I would work Mondays to Fridays, but might be called upon to fill in on weekends if the other cashier didn't show up—which, by the way he was telling it to me, seemed like a regular occurrence. He asked me how I was for cash and if I needed an advance before the end of the week, and I gratefully nodded; the money that my grandfather had sent me with was all but gone, and I had hated eating Zoe's food and drinking her tea and not being able to pay for any of it. I wanted to wander the city again on my own, but hadn't even been able to buy a Metro ticket.

Halfway through my first day, I knew that I would probably hate this job. There was, indeed, nothing really in it to like—except for the niceness of Mathias and the downtime I had during which I could learn at least five new French words. Also, I didn't have to pay for lunch, and Mathias even said he'd let me take something home for dinner every night. He had offered me, that first day, half of his sandwich—a baguette filled with thin rounds of sausage, forgetting for a moment that I was a Muslim and that pork was our poison. He quickly pulled his plate back in front of him when I pointed this out and promised it would never happen again.

While I wanted the day to end so I could leave, I also resisted going to my new home, a place I would share with three girls who were strangers to me, showing up there with a battered brown suitcase like a refugee in an old war movie, having them inspect me up and down to determine if I was worthy enough to share their space. They weren't even friends of Shazia's. She had only described them as "people I know through other people," which had made no sense to me at all.

But Zoe had wanted her couch back, Shazia was gone, my return ticket had lapsed, and I didn't have a choice.

* * *

They were all there by the time I arrived, all of them in various states of undress, munching potato chips and drinking Coke, the smell of something cooking in the kitchen greeting me as I walked through the door. They were all effusive and welcoming, which surprised me, their eyes bright and arms open, as if they had been waiting for a roommate just like me.

Karla was from Haiti—tall and black and lean, her hair in braids around a long, pretty face. Juliette was blond, smaller, and quieter, clad only in a long white cotton T-shirt with a large yellow smiley face on its front. Teresa was a full-figured redhead, a sprinkling of freckles spread across her wide face and over the shoulders and arms that were visible above a pink terrycloth towel.

I was to share a bedroom—one of two in the flat—with Teresa, who had been looking for a roommate since the old one moved out, apparently to go and live with her boyfriend. There was only one bathroom for all of us, which meant showers expected to last longer than fifteen minutes had to be booked in advance. There was a routine of sorts, and I was expected to fit into it unquestioningly: Karla was a freelance journalist who wrote at home and was often out on assignment, but her schedule was the most flexible of all. Juliette was a receptionist at a fashion house and had to be out by eight most mornings, so allowances should be made for that. Teresa had two jobs, both of them as a waitress, while she was waiting for her big break to become, as she put it, "the next Audrey Tautou."

They told me all this breathlessly while I was still standing in the hallway, my suitcase in my hand. They said that my cousin had come to see the place and to meet them on my behalf, and had determined that I would be happy here. Then Juliette turned toward a desk in the corner and handed me a white envelope that she fished out from one of its drawers. It was a note from Shazia, informing me that she had already paid the first month's rent, that it was her gift to me, her way to wish me well.

"Don't think I'll forget about you now that I've returned to L.A.," she had written in tiny, circular words. *"I'll be checking up on you, and you know how to reach me, if ever you need me. It's all going to be gorgeous. Trust me."*

I folded up the note and slipped it into my purse, wondering what Shazia must have been really thinking when she wrote it, and what I must have been thinking when I let her talk me into this.

Chapter Nine

For someone who had barely left Mahim, I was adjusting reasonably well, finding that sticking to a schedule helped me to retain my sanity. Mathias was very kind to me, which I had always assumed a boss would never be. The work itself was dull, but the enthusiasm with which he greeted me every day made up for it. It was nice, after nineteen years of not really being seen, to finally feel welcomed somewhere.

The girls with whom I now lived seemed to answer to nobody, except occasionally one another, but they had no nagging parents or grandparents calling them, asking them where they were, what they were doing. They had furnished me with a list of written rules the day I moved in, at the top of which, in screaming black felt-tip, was the directive: NO MEN OVERNIGHT! I hesitated to tell them that as far as I was concerned, they had little to worry about. The refrigerator had been separated into four different zones, and I was allotted a reasonable space on the second shelf, as well as one of the drawers. Everyone bought, ate, and monitored her own food. It didn't matter, Teresa explained to me, who earned what; everyone was responsible for herself and contributed equally to the upkeep of the apartment. I came to assume that this was how young women outside India lived, and as startled as I was by it, I fell into line.

A week into my new job, Mathias told me that his little café had been hired to provide the refreshments for an event and asked if I would agree to help serve. Working as a waitress was something else that well-born Muslim girls didn't do. But I was already so far gone. So I agreed and, to my horror, Mathias pulled out a short black dress that had arrived in a box, then unfolded a small white lace apron and matching hat.

"Here, wear this," he said, thrusting it into my hands. Answering the curious look on my face, he replied: "The client wants all the girls to dress like French maids. Bah, it's *stupide*, but we do what they ask, no?"

Along with the three other girls from the café, I changed into the ensemble, pulling on a pair of black fishnet tights that had also been provided, and choosing from an assortment of white shoes that had also been sent. When I emerged from the small lavatory, Mathias cast an approving eye up and down my body and let out a whistle.

"I didn't know you had those curves under your big *exotique* clothes," he said as I hid self-consciously behind a table.

The event, as it turned out, was a small fashion show, held as part of a weeklong series of shows all over the city. They were called the *defiles,* and everyone from our van driver to the policeman who stopped us for speeding seemed aware that Paris comes alive in that week, even more than it usually is. This particular fashion company had decided to book a dark nightclub in an obscure part of town, finding the cheapest way to show the designer's first collection. Although the fishnet tights were beginning to itch and the lace hat was scratching into my scalp, I couldn't help but feel a little excited at the prospect of watching my first fashion show, and I hoped I would be able to catch glimpses of it during the passing out of palm-size bottles of champagne and little cheese-filled pastries.

Despite a light drizzle and a cool breeze, there was already a crowd waiting outside the nightclub. Mathias was shown the back entrance and was told where to set up. We walked down a wet alley, through a metal door that was painted red, and down another hallway and into the club's kitchen. We hurriedly set out the pastries on silver trays, speared toothpicks through olives, and lifted dozens of bottles of champagne out of ice-filled chests. I heard people come in through the main entrance and take their seats, shuffling in the darkened interior of the club, the buzz of a foreign language filling the air.

Mathias turned to greet Bruno, the designer, with a kiss on each cheek. There were superlatives thrown out, words like *magnifique* and *merveilleux,* about nothing in particular.

Bruno had dyed his hair a bright red, like pictures I had seen a long time ago of clowns in a circus. He had a small silver hoop pierced through an eyebrow, and I noticed another one in his tongue as he spoke to Mathias. A short-sleeved black shirt revealed a dark green tattoo, and beads of sweat covered his forehead. He was talking quickly, nervously, giving Mathias instructions and sizing each one of us up. Then he turned and left.

"He will give himself a heart attack," Mathias said to me. "So agitated. The girls from *Vogue* are coming, and important stylists. I told him to have some champagne, relax. But of course, he cannot. He is showing couture style on hand-picked models—twenty-two outfits on twenty-two girls, like Galliano in his early days." Mathias told me all this as if I would understand, forgetting that until today, I had never before seen a man with his hair dyed bright red.

In less than fifteen minutes, the curtain was due to go up. I peeked out of the kitchen and saw photographers, their cameras slung across necks and shoulders, clustered at one side of a dance floor. Leading to the dance floor was a sloping ramp, covered in plastic. Lights were being tested overhead and music—which Mathias had described as "garage techno funk"—was piercing through speakers on all sides. The people sitting in the front-row seats were smartly dressed, those standing at the back were scruffier. They were holding folders and notebooks and pens, chatting with one another or staring straight ahead. One of the other girls was serving drinks, but Bruno had instructed us to wait until after the show, when there would be a small party, to bring out the rest. He had told Mathias that if there were promises of nourishment afterward, people would stay till the end, no matter how bad the clothes were. Mathias told me that Bruno didn't have a lot of self-confidence, which might have explained the self-inflicted mutilation of the piercings and tattoo.

I suddenly heard a crash from the area behind the dance floor ramp where the girls were getting ready. I followed Mathias back there and saw a beautiful brunette, all long limbs and teased hair and painted nails, sprawled on the floor, pulling her knee up to her chest and wailing like a child.

"Ouch, shit!" she screamed, in a distinctly British accent. "I think I sprained my bleeding ankle. Damn these shoes!"

On her feet was a pair of sparkling sandals with pin-thin, four-inch heels. All the girls were wearing them, and I was surprised that the brunette was the only one to have fallen over as a result. Bruno was cradling her head and yelling at someone to fetch some ice, someone else to bring a bandage. The girl was still screaming.

"I can't go on," she cried. "I can't even stand up!"

Bruno dropped her head and covered his face with his hands. Mathias stooped down to comfort him, as did the rest of the fashion team, while the model continued to yelp in pain, nobody paying any attention to her. I looked over at Mathias questioningly, who hurriedly whispered to me again that Bruno had created exactly twenty-two outfits for twenty-two different models, and that this had been boasted of in the program notes that his guests were, at this very moment, perusing.

"It is his gimmick for the season," said Mathias. "He cannot go back on it now. People will definitely notice. It has been in all the press."

I had moved over to the girl to ask what I could do to help her, when Bruno yanked me up by my elbow.

"Oui, ça suffit," he said, looking me over and pulling the lace cap off my head. "You," he continued, staring straight at me. "I no speak good Eenglish, but you be *mannequin* to-day."

Mathias stepped in, arguing with Bruno. But after a minute of that, my boss turned to me.

"Tanaya, I am sorry, but he is insisting. He says you are the prettiest girl here. I know you have never done it. But it is only one outfit, and all you must do is walk slowly, smile, turn around, come back. Simple. It is over in a minute, and I will have helped an old friend. You will be compensated. Please?"

Ten minutes later, the French maid's outfit had been stripped off me, and I was waiting to be dressed.

Chapter Ten

The item was small, tucked away on page four, and would not have caught my eye were it not for the photograph: a small, grainy black-and-white shot of a girl who looked suspiciously like me.

Mathias was peering over my shoulder. He pointed at the photo and yelped loudly. *"C'est toi!* That's you!" he said. "Gorgeous!"

He snatched the newspaper out of my hands and started to read from it aloud in French before translating for my benefit.

"It says here the show last night was a big success, everyone loved Bruno's clothes, that he will be the next big fashion star. And then they mention you, a young Muslim waitress who has never modeled before, rushed onto the catwalk. They say here you were not bad, quite good actually, maybe it's a new career for you. You look good here, no?" Mathias said, pointing to the photograph again.

"Ah, but this newspaper, it's a small one, not famous, *pas du tout*," he said, looking at the front page. "Nobody will see it, unfortunately. Such a shame."

When I had returned home the night before, my eyes still rimmed with thick black liner, my hair still stiff and coiled and smelling of chemicals, my roommates squealed in surprise. When I told them what had happened, they listened to every word in silence, their only sounds being the crunching of toffee-coated peanuts that sat in a bowl on the coffee table. After I had finished recounting the hysteria of a couple of hours earlier, they squealed some more.

"Yes, but how did you *feel*?" asked Teresa. "Were you nervous?"

"To begin with, yes, of course. But after a few seconds — maybe less — it became easier."

In truth, the previous night had been perhaps the most exciting of my life. Walking down the runway had been the shortest sixty seconds of my life, and also the longest. When it was beginning, I couldn't wait for it to end, but once I had taken my final twirl, mimicking the girls who had gone before me, I wished I could do it again. It had been a moment of pure frivolity and spontaneity, two things I had never experienced before. I longed to call my grandfather and tell him about my night. But instead I told three girls who were still strangers to me.

✳   ✳   ✳

Bruno, the designer, sent me flowers at work the next day. I could barely read the scrawl on the tiny card that accompanied it, and wouldn't have been able to understand it anyway, so Mathias deciphered and translated for me.

"*'With all my heart I thank you for your bravery,'*" Mathias recited. I thought Bruno's words were dramatic, as if I had rescued someone from a burning building. "*Your willingness to model my creations saved my show. If there is anything I may ever do for you, you have only to ask.'*"

"Sweet," said Mathias, looking up. "He sounds most grateful. I am certain that Bruno will give you some free clothes whenever you'd like."

I thought back to the pink hot pants he'd put me in and confessed I could do without.

With the tidy little bonus I had received from Bruno, I decided to spend a beautiful Sunday on my own, exploring the city again. I set off from the apartment just after breakfast, carrying with me a packed lunch and a copy of *Elle* that I had borrowed from Juliette, who tended to pilfer magazines from the fashion house she worked for.

I took the Metro to Place de la Concorde and made my way into the Jardin des Tuileries, which I had first visited with Shazia during my first few weeks here. I found a stone bench that was empty, set down my things, and took in the glorious morning. Joggers sprinted by, and mothers wheeled their babies in strollers. There was a clear crispness in the air, as if the world had overnight been cleansed of all its troubles and was suddenly sparkling new again. I took a deep breath, wanting to feel as invigorated as the atmosphere. I had nowhere to be and nothing to do and realized as I sat there that the heaviness and loneliness I had been feeling since Shazia had left was slowly starting to lift. Not a day passed when I didn't think of Nana and my mother or when I wouldn't yearn for a platter of *bhel puri* from a Mahim street vendor or hope to walk into a community gathering and hear the tinkling of glass bangles and the familiar rustle of silk saris.

But I was beginning to feel happy and at home. I took out my purse and counted, again, the two hundred euros that Bruno had paid me, shoving it into my palm as if it were a tip. I knew the other models had received far more, but they were professionals, and I was simply a cashier who happened to be tall and slim and there.

After an hour of sitting on the bench, during which I had barely flicked through the pages of the magazine I had brought along, I decided to start walking again. I emerged through the gates of the gardens and, not quite sure where I was going next, crossed the street. I was standing in front of the imposing Hotel InterContinental, a palace of a place that I had walked past many times but had never had the temerity to enter. A pair of uniformed doormen stood on each side of the huge arched entrance, themselves almost dwarfed by ornate golden lamps. Each person passing through the doors seemed more beautiful and glamorous than the last. I glanced down at the brown paper bag I had in my right hand, inside it my modest lunch of a cheese and tomato sandwich and an apple, and tossed it into a nearby trash can.

I took another deep breath, adjusted my *dupatta,* smoothed down my hair, and walked in.

Chapter Eleven

The crystal chandeliers overhead glinted in the sunlight, the marble floors and pillars polished to perfection. The lobby seemed unusually busy for a Sunday morning, and then I realized why: a board announcing that day's events and functions listed a fashion show that, according to my watch, had just ended.

I found an empty armchair in the lobby and sunk into it. I looked completely out of place, swaddled in voluminous clothes where everyone else looked defined, silhouetted against a beautiful backdrop. Crowds of people began to emerge from one of the rooms in the back, carrying programs and chattering excitedly. There were hundreds of them, far more than had been at Bruno's a few nights before, and not a server in a French maid's uniform to be found among them. I wished, for a moment, to have seen what they had just seen.

A waiter approached me and asked if I would like to order anything. I looked at the menu he showed me and realized that if I wanted the money to last me the rest of the month, I could maybe afford an espresso.

"Bon," he said with a quick nod of his head.

The lobby went quickly quiet, with only small pockets of people clustered here and there, discussing the show. Two American girls were talking about a lilac chiffon gown as if it were the Shroud of Turin, marveling at its perfection.

Then I saw the models leaving, all of them lithe and willowy, their hair in neat chignons, subdued makeup on their pretty faces, looking every inch like I always imagined models would, one of them a dazzling redhead I even recognized from the cover of the magazine I was carrying. This must have been quite a show.

I took careful, slow sips of my espresso, wanting to savor every drop, aware that this was the only indulgence I was going to allow myself there. As the crowds in the lobby thinned out, I noticed that I was being stared at by a balding, dark-skinned man who was seated on a couch a few feet away. He didn't smile, had no expression on his face, but his eyes were glued to me as if he were blind and didn't know where he was looking. I had grown accustomed to being noticed in Paris, attributing it mostly to my clumsy Indian attire, although Mathias frequently told me that my looks had something to do with it. But usually someone would gawk and then look away again as soon as I noticed. This man just kept on staring.

Suddenly feeling uncomfortable, I decided it was time

to leave. I paid the bill, gathered up my things, and walked quickly to the front of the hotel, trying to decide which direction to turn in. I made a right and headed back toward the Tuileries, thinking that if I was ambitious and energetic enough, I might continue on in that direction to the Left Bank and perhaps even return home on foot.

After five minutes of walking, something told me to turn around. The man from the hotel was behind me, his pace quickening to catch up to mine, leading me to speed up. He was taller and thinner than he looked back at the hotel, and he was far too well-dressed to be trailing a girl across Paris like some ruffian at night.

"Stop!" he said. "Please! I mean no harm. Please."

We were on the rue de Rivoli, surrounded by tourists, so against my better judgment I came to a standstill and turned to face him as he caught up with me.

"Thank you," he said, catching his breath. He spoke in accented English, but I knew it wasn't French. Somehow, I found that comforting—that he was an alien here, just like me. "You walk fast," he gasped.

"I thought you were chasing me. What do you want?"

He reached into the breast pocket of his jacket, pulled out a name card, and handed it to me: DIMITRI MAROUNIS, VICE PRESIDENT, it said, and beneath it the name of a company with three different addresses.

I looked up at him, still puzzled.

"I am a scout," he said. "It's my job to find new talent. I saw you sitting there, and I thought that if you weren't already a model, you should be. Are you? If so, to whom are you signed?"

"You are mistaken," I said. "I am in Paris for just a short while and will then return to India. I have no interest in modeling, but I thank you." I turned around to resume my walk home.

"But madam," he said, stopping me. "You are a striking young woman. You could become very rich doing this if you would let me help you. We'll start by getting some photos taken. I will help you through the whole process, and—"

I interrupted him mid-sentence. "I don't believe you fully understood me," I said. "I have no interest. But thank you."

Shoving his card into my bag, I turned around again and headed home, leaving him standing there.

The next evening as I was showing my roommates how to prepare lamb curry, the doorbell rang. Juliette went to answer it and returned accompanied by a young man who looked like he had come from my part of the world.

"Miss Tanaya?" he asked, staring at me blankly.

"Yes?"

"My name is Sumeet. Mina Husain asked me to bring you these."

He stepped aside, and I saw behind him three boxes, each addressed to me care of Aunt Mina.

I knew exactly what they were. My grandfather's handwriting was immediately recognizable. I used to joke to

Nilu that all my belongings in the world would easily fit into three small boxes, which were now positioned in front of me.

Once Sumeet left, the girls helped me open them up. Inside were all my clothes, the ones I used to wear when chasing the children of our building up and down the stone stairs; my leather *chappals* that I frayed walking back and forth to the market; the books that kept me company during my lonely nights.

At the top of the second box was an envelope, with my name written flawlessly on the front. Even at his angriest, my grandfather always had exceptional penmanship. A letter was carefully folded inside.

Tanaya,

You were supposed to return after two weeks in Paris. It has now been two months. I told you on the phone that you were dead to me, that you could never return home. Yet I waited. I thought perhaps someone had cursed you with insanity, but that you would eventually recover and come home to beg forgiveness, which I would have gradually given you. But now, too much time has passed. You are, I have realized, not insane. Instead, you are a horrible and shameless girl. I do not know what has come over you, and when Allah finally takes me to paradise, I still will not know. But here are your things. Having them around is nothing more than a painful reminder of your presence. You have crushed me, Tanaya. It is like you were never even my child.

My hands were shaking as I held the single piece of paper with which my beloved grandfather had effectively ended my life. The girls looked at me questioningly, and then one by one seemed to grasp what had happened and what the contents of that letter were. Karla opened up the last box, atop which rested my parents' wedding photograph, the one I used to sneak into our room to look at. Affixed to the back with a piece of Scotch tape was a small note from my mother.

Your grandfather asked if there was anything I wanted to send you, as my way to say good-bye. I could think only of this photo, which always seems to have meant something to you. I am crying as I write this, because I am seeing that of all the tragedies and disappointments in my life, you, my Tanaya, are the greatest.

Chapter Twelve

There should have been something more to her voice, a sympathetic tone, a shared sense of loss and regret.

But instead, Shazia just sounded like herself: defiant and devil-may-care.

I had been crying for most of the thirty minutes that I had been on the phone with her, grateful at least that she had called me and not the other way around.

"Up until yesterday, I really thought that when I went back home, they would forgive me and take me back in," I sobbed. "But this, what they have done, it is so final." I envisioned my grandfather, his white kurta clinging to his lean frame, out in the street in front of our building, disposing of all the things they had chosen not to send me: my old schoolbooks, my hair barrettes, some bottles of nail polish I had bought right before leaving for Paris and had inadvertently left behind—all the things I had hoped, someday, to go back to.

But Shazia seemed to understand none of this, instead

telling me that I was "better off without them," that if they chose not to accept my choices, then they didn't deserve to have me in the family. To me, she was talking nonsense. She kept wanting to change the subject, to ask me about what else I had been up to in Paris, and would no doubt have shrieked in delight had I told her about my foray on a fashion catwalk just a couple of weeks earlier. Family had been everything to me, and I was blaming Shazia.

"It's easy for you to say it doesn't matter," I said, bitterness filling my voice. "You might only understand how I'm feeling if *your* mother had turned her back on you, telling you that you may as well be dead."

There was a pause before Shazia quietly said: "She did."

"What?"

"I never told you this, but once I left Paris to come to live in L.A., my mother eventually sent me everything I'd left behind, and a note telling me never to return home. It seems melodrama runs in the family," she said, laughing weakly.

"So what happened?" I asked. "What made her change her mind?"

"Fear. She found out she was sick, and I was the first person she called. There's nothing like death to make you long for someone you suddenly think you can't live without. So you see, Tanaya, I *do* know what it's like. Being disowned is not always an absolute. It may feel like the end of the world now. But believe me, when the time is right, you'll be one big happy family again."

❃   ❃   ❃

It wasn't until I was emptying out my handbag the next morning that I found his name card. Until I saw it again, lodged in the bottom of my bag and entangled in an empty cellophane sandwich wrapper, I had forgotten about the well-dressed gentleman who had approached me on the street that Sunday, who seemed to think that I had more to offer the world of modeling than a minute on a catwalk in a darkened nightclub, done under duress. I also pulled out from my bag the copy of the newspaper that had my photograph in it, the one that had Mathias all excited until he realized that nobody would ever see it. I glanced at Dimitri's name card and realized that, for the first time in my life, I truly had nothing to lose.

Just to be sure I was in the right place, I looked up at the numbers atop the building in front of me and matched them to the address on the card. It didn't seem to fit. The card was heavy and formal, the letters on it thick and embossed, like some of the wedding invitations that would arrive at Nana's house when I was still living there, signaling occasions that were grand and regal.

I had expected the same from Dimitri's offices based on the quality of his name card, so was surprised to find a very modest building in front of me—a narrow, dirty glass door the only thing separating it from the street, a rack of dark stairs leading to the upper floors. There was no indication outside that these were offices, or that a talent agency was one of them. I hadn't called Dimitri before coming, which may have been my mistake. My shift had ended early, and I had simply decided on the spur of the moment to come and talk to him, assuming that he would be around and available. A sequence of events had convinced me to do so: The girls had told me that the landlord was raising the rent and we would all equally have to share the increased financial burden, and Mathias had informed me that a recently graduated cousin of his would be joining me in my cashier duties, taking some of my hours and, consequently, some of my pay.

"That's OK," I had said to Mathias when he told me. "I believe that there is enough for everyone." He had looked relieved. Karla was taking on every freelance project thrown her way, convinced that she couldn't afford to turn down assignments. Teresa had offered to find me extra work, most likely at night in one of the restaurants she worked in as a waitress.

It was at that point, when Teresa wanted me to wear an apron with her and serve aperitifs all night, that Juliette chimed in with her own solution.

"Modeling," she had said. "You did it once, and it didn't kill you. I think you should try it again. If you make enough money doing that, we can all quit our jobs," she said, laughing. "Believe me, most girls become models because they have a burning desire to do so, or are terribly vain by nature. For you, it is just for the money. And it is *much* more fun than picking up somebody's dirty dishes, yes?"

Encouraged by the other girls, I was standing in front of Dimitri's building, wondering if I had made some awful mistake.

I pulled open the door and walked up the stairs, careful to hike up my scarf so it wouldn't trail on the dirty floor. I climbed two flights before I saw a small sign outside a door on my right: MAROUNIS GLOBAL ENTERTAINMENT. Underneath was written NEW YORK. PARIS. BEIJING. A man's voice came through the door, a stream of shouted words broken with a laugh. I knocked quietly, uncertainly. I heard a pause, and then a grim *"Entrez!"* I jiggled the doorknob until it finally turned, opened the door, and found myself in Marounis Global Entertainment, a room no larger than my apartment, with one balding man (Dimitri) on the phone at a solitary desk. He was dressed in a faded blue T-shirt, a cigarette dangling from two fingers. Behind him, suspended from a hanger, was the suit he had worn the week before when I had first met him. It was, I realized, his "scouting suit," the one that made him look like a real businessman with a real business.

As soon as he saw me, a look of astonished recognition came over his face. He whispered something hurriedly to the person on the other end of the phone and hung up.

"I think I have made a mistake," I stammered. "I didn't mean to come here. Sorry if I've disturbed you."

I turned around and reached for the door, but Dimitri yelled out to me.

"Wait!" he shouted. "I remember you—the girl from the

86

hotel. I'm so glad you have come. You should have phoned. I could have met you somewhere else."

He caught me looking around the room, and he suddenly appeared ashamed. "Please, sit," he said, sweeping an empty pizza box off a chair and onto the floor. "You've come all this way. Please."

I took a seat and looked up at him expectantly.

"I get this reaction often," he said. "The name of my company sounds very impressive. Then people come here and see it is one person in an office. I have just started this business," he explained.

"And do you really have offices in New York and Beijing?" I asked.

"Yes," he replied. "I have a cousin in each city, and they do the same thing there. OK, they have their offices in their bedrooms," he said with a laugh. "But look," he said, leaping out from behind his desk and reaching for a thick photo album that sat on a shelf above his head. He leafed through its pages, stopping at one and turning the book around to show me: It was a faraway shot of a dimly lit stage, atop which were a string of thin girls in brightly colored evening gowns.

"This was a fashion show in China, and we found all the models in Europe," he said. "They wanted foreign girls, and we could provide them. And see, here," he said, opening the book to another page, containing a large black-and-white photo of a beautiful girl lying in a field. "That's Nadia. I spotted her, like I did with you. She was on the

Metro. A student, so very pretty. Now she is doing some shows in Milan. Small ones, but she's happy, and we are earning a little commission also."

He shut the book, satisfied that he had vindicated himself. "I never asked you your name," he said, offering me a cigarette.

"Tanaya. It's Urdu. I'm Muslim," I replied, feeling the need to immediately identify myself.

"Bravo!" he exclaimed, clapping his hands together. "I don't know of a single other Muslim model working in Paris, or in fact in all of Europe. You know, Muslims are hot right now." He grinned.

"I don't know what you mean."

"I mean in movies, and music, and books—everything to do with Islam seems very popular, like people everywhere are craving an understanding of such a mysterious religion. I think when people find out that you are Muslim, they will love it. It will be in all the news. And that will make your job as a new fashion model so much easier." He nodded sagely, as if his work was done.

He opened a drawer and pulled out two pieces of paper, stapled together at one corner.

"This is a standard contract," he said. "It's exactly what all the top agencies in Paris use. Only, because we are not so established, our commission is less. You pay me only ten percent of any modeling job you have, starting from the time you sign. Believe me, it is a good deal. Other agencies charge more than double that."

I looked over the contract, which was bilingual, and realized I didn't even understand the English part of it. It was something that my grandfather would have been able to help me with, or Shazia. But seeing as neither one of them was around, I settled on the next best option and told Dimitri that I would take the contract home.

The girls weren't that much help. While Karla said that the terms of the contract were standard and that I would be protected, Juliette sniffed at the mention of a modeling agent she had never heard of before, and Teresa thought that I should leap at the opportunity.

"If you give me a few days, I'm sure I can find you a contact at one of the bigger and better modeling agencies in Paris," Juliette advised. "I work in fashion," she said of her receptionist job. "I know those people."

She may have been right, but I felt a queer loyalty to the bald little Greek man who had followed me down the street one day and offered me the chance of a lifetime.

"This man is willing to take a chance on me," I said to Juliette. "Maybe his office is small and nobody knows him, but he seemed kind. I think I will go ahead and do it."

Chapter Thirteen

From the day that I signed and returned the contract to an ecstatic Dimitri, who proudly labeled me "number five" in his small coterie of models, I waited for something to happen. I wasn't quite sure what, exactly: Dimitri had been vague about what to expect next, saying only that he would call me if there was a casting I would be suitable for. He had, in the meantime, arranged to have some photos taken of me. Juliette had said that these things normally happen in a studio, where I would be surrounded by hair and makeup artists, bright lights, and a team of people headed up by a fast-talking photographer. I was instead asked to stand in a corner at Dimitri's office while a young Slovakian man who spoke no English clicked away with exactly the same Konica camera that my grandfather had had for twenty years. I brushed my own hair, applied some lipstick, and Dimitri told me to pout into the camera, goldfish-style.

"Headshot only," he said, to no one in particular. "You

cannot be photographed from the neck down until you have something more stylish on. Your ensembles are beguiling, but nobody will understand them."

He took the roll of film from the young photographer, plopped it into his pocket, and said: "Now, we wait."

So I went on as if nothing had changed, working in the café, cooking for the girls, behaving as if my family hadn't disowned me and as if I had never worn pink hot pants under a steaming hot spotlight.

When Dimitri did finally call me, I could tell that he was forcing himself to sound enthusiastic.

"You will *love* this," he said. "And the clients—very important fashion company—they will *love* you. I am sure of it. They have already booked you based on your headshot alone, for their new campaign. Are you available at three this afternoon?"

When I asked Mathias if I could go, he hugged me.

"I knew you would get your big break!" he said. "Who is it? Dior? Chanel? This is going to be wonderful, so exciting. I hear these shoots are amazing—champagne to relax you, a gorgeous spread if you are hungry, fun music to set the mood. You will be draped in chiffon and silk. You will feel like a star. I wonder who will be shooting you today . . . maybe Mario Testino? I heard he was in town. Oh, that would be something!"

I looked at him puzzled, his blue eyes shining with laughter.

"Off you go," he said. "Enjoy."

* * *

Dimitri asked me to meet him at the Metro station closest to him. We jumped on the next train, and as we rumbled through the underground tunnels of Paris, it was too noisy to talk. He took me by the hand when we arrived at our destination, led me up a flight of dank stairs, past a man playing the viola, and back up into daylight. I had no idea where we were, having never been to this part of Paris before. We turned a corner into a narrow side street and up another flight of stairs into a short building. Along the way I noticed dozens of people pushing along racks of clothing — sequined gowns and lace pants and checked suits — all covered in filmy cellophane and hung from steel poles. I guessed that this was what Juliette meant when she referred to "the world of fashion."

In a second-floor office, we were greeted by a sullen receptionist who looked me over a couple of times and then pointed to the back with her thumb. Dimitri accompanied me to a room, empty but for a changing screen, a full-length mirror, and a couple of freestanding lights. A heavyset woman with red hair, round glasses, and protruding teeth walked in, shook hands with Dimitri, and looked me over as the receptionist had done. Draped over her arm were several hangers of clothes, and she flung them at me and told me to get behind the screen and put the first one on. I looked over at Dimitri, who nodded.

Behind the screen, there was nowhere to hang anything, so I let the entire lot fall onto the floor. I picked up a brown suit that, when I put it on, seemed to fit well, although it scratched me around the collar and under the arms. I stepped out from behind the screen, and the red-haired woman nodded approvingly, giving me half a smile. From a bag she was carrying, she pulled out a pair of sheer black knee-high stockings and flat black shoes and told me to put them on. She asked me if I had brought a hairbrush or any makeup, and I shook my head. The scowl returned, and then she turned around and yelled out something to someone in another room. A petite girl came scurrying in, holding a comb in one hand and a small makeup kit in another, and in under five minutes gave me a ponytail, false lashes, and bright red lips. I didn't know much about fashion, but I did know that I didn't look very good, but Dimitri only smiled and repeated, *"Jolie, jolie,"* as if in so doing I would, indeed, suddenly become pretty again. The red-haired woman nodded, shoved the other girl out of the way and, from yet another bag, pulled out a camera. Moving back a few feet, she asked me to pose in different ways—arms folded in front, one hand on waist, too much smile, too little smile—and made me repeat it all until, eleven outfits and two hours later, we were done.

"Where's Mario Testino?" I asked Dimitri, as I peeled off the stockings for the last time. "Mathias said maybe he would be photographing me today?"

Dimitri and the redhead looked at each other and laughed.

"Who you think you are?" the woman said, speaking

English for the first time. "'eidi Klum? You think I could get 'eidi Klum for one hundred euros? Bah!" She laughed again, now lighting up a cigarette. With her free hand, she gave Dimitri an envelope, through which I could see several currency notes. He shoved it into his pocket, helped me gather the crumpled heap of clothes on the floor, shook the redhead's hand again, and escorted me out. She completely ignored me, with not so much as a *"merci."*

On the landing outside, Dimitri took out ten euros from the envelope, put it into his wallet, and handed me the rest.

"It is not much, but it is a good start for your new career," he said. "Maybe next time, I can get you more. But you will be able to see these pictures, and to tell your friends. They are for this company's catalog on its Web site. It will reach many people, and then we will see what other good jobs will come our way."

"That's it?!" Juliette exclaimed when I got home and told her about my afternoon. "So much time and fuss for a hundred euros? I *told* you not to go with this guy. I *told* you to hold out for something better."

"I am new to this," I said sheepishly. "It is fine as a place to begin."

"Well I can assure you that when Naomi Campbell was first starting out, she didn't have to subject herself to such humiliation. Pictures on a Web site for some line of clothing in Sentier that nobody has ever heard of? What was Dimitri thinking? This is your reputation! These are things you can never take back! When you become famous, it will haunt you!"

"Everyone has to start somewhere," I said.

When Dimitri called the next morning to tell me about another job he had lined up for me, Juliette answered the phone.

"Tanaya is doing no such thing," she said, resolutely. "I am in the fashion business, and I will not permit her to degrade herself this way. She is too beautiful and unique to end up in the awful ads you are finding for her. If you don't get her something good soon, I will insist that she terminate her contract with you and find a more superior agency." With that, I heard Juliette slamming the phone down, and I quietly said farewell to my newfound modeling career.

Dimitri didn't call for a week after that, and I suspected I would never hear from him again. But then he came by the café, just as I was ringing up a takeaway purchase of an Artois and a goat-cheese salad. I felt embarrassed to see him, a little ashamed of the way Juliette had spoken to him. He was a boss to me, although Juliette wasted no time in telling me that it was, actually, he who worked for me.

"One day," he said, approaching my little corner of the café, "you will not have to rely on this job anymore. One day, I promise you, you will have enough to buy this place if you wanted."

"It's OK, Dimitri," I said quietly. "You don't have to make all these promises to me. Unlike you, I don't expect miracles. I am trying to be happy as I am."

"Well," he said, taking a deep breath. "Things are about to change, so prepare yourself."

If Allah was still a witness to my life, I would say that what happened next was a blessing from him. But given that—if I believed my nana—our Almighty was no longer a part of my existence, I had no choice but to concede that what then transpired was mere coincidence, nothing more than me being in the right place at the right time.

Viva, the clothing line that I had modeled for on my first assignment with Dimitri, was apparently up for sale. Dimitri became more and more excited as he began to tell me the news: that although Viva looked like some slipshod operation, it actually sold millions of dollars' worth of clothes every year, that it was in all the stores and appealed to ordinary women and was a huge moneymaker. That the red-haired woman with the protruding teeth was actually considered one of the smartest people in the business, pinching pennies wherever she could and selling a fortune in clothes.

A fashion tycoon who was interested in acquiring Viva had gone onto its Web site. And there, just days after I had those photographs taken, were pictures of me, smiling nervously into the camera, wearing those sheer knee-high stockings and flat black shoes.

"It seems that he really liked what he saw," Dimitri said. "He thought that the quality of the pictures was awful, and the clothes selected could have been better. But he liked the look of you," Dimitri said quietly, rummaging through his breast pocket for his cigarette case. "If they go ahead and buy Viva, they want to make it a very multicultural label, and he thinks you represent that look well. He called me earlier today. He wants to meet with you tonight."

Karla loaned me a red dress with a V-neck and a ruffle at the hem, Juliette styled my hair into a loose knot, and Teresa strapped some high-heeled shoes onto my feet. Then the three of them came in a taxi with me to the Hôtel Costes, which they had told me was the trendiest hotel in Paris.

"I can't believe you are meeting with one of the key people from Groupe Montaigne," Juliette said knowledgeably. "They own *everything*. You know that brand Gilles Montaigne? Well, that was their first. And then came the beauty brand Lulu Cosmetiques and the shoe line Casanova, and a chain of spas around Europe . . . it is endless. I am surprised they want to buy Viva, but perhaps I shouldn't be. After all, if it is a moneymaker . . ." Her voice trailed off as I stopped listening. None of this meant anything to me, and I found it very hard to get excited about something I had no connection with. It was a bunch of names, as foreign-sounding now as they might have been when I first got to Paris. But Juliette had given me her approval and agreed that I could grant Dimitri a second chance.

My roommates waved good-bye to me as I stepped out of the taxi and into the hotel, which I found strangely dark for a place where people went if they wanted to be seen. Dimitri said he would meet me at seven, along with the man who could potentially be my new boss.

Fifteen minutes after the appointed hour, I was still waiting.

I took a table in a corner and asked for a glass of orange juice, as everyone else around me sipped pink liquids and ice-filled golden nectars from V-shaped glasses. Compared to them, dressed in their own clothes, conversing animatedly with one another, perfectly at ease in this world, I felt something of an imposter. I glanced around the room nervously, wishing I had brought something to read, then realized that I would also have required a miniature flashlight had I done so.

Opposite me, I noticed that I was being stared at. A beautiful Asian woman, dressed in black, was drinking champagne, smiling my way. I genially smiled back before reaching for a plate of stuffed olives in front of me.

Twenty-five minutes later, I was still waiting and had decided that I would give them five more minutes and then leave. The Asian woman slowly got up from the couch, straightened her long black dress, and glided over to me.

"Bonsoir," she said, extending her hand. *"Je m'appelle Claudine. Et vous êtes?"*

"Sorry, not so good at French," I said, swallowing a piece of pimento.

"Oh, not a local, then?" she asked in perfect, untainted English. "In that case, my name is Claire. Claudine just sounds better in these parts when you're dealing with these people. May I sit?"

She slid into the chair next to me and placed her beaded handbag onto the table. In the candlelit darkness of the room, her skin looked incandescent.

"I saw you sitting here on your own and thought I should come over and say hello. Are you alone?" she asked, bending her head close to mine. I had once seen a show on television in India about women like this, women who preferred other women. Faced with it now, I was terrified.

"I'm actually waiting for someone," I replied. "Two men," I felt compelled to add.

A smile appeared on Claire's face.

"Good. That's just what I thought," she said. "Perhaps we can team up?"

"I don't know what you're talking about," I said. "I am waiting to meet with two men, for my work."

She smiled once more, and lifted her hand so it rested on my shoulder.

"I manage a small group," she said. "Very beautiful, cultured women only. And our clients are in the most upper classes—wealthy, powerful, highly accomplished. They need to be seen with only the very best women. I'm going with two of them to Monte Carlo next week, to attend a party being hosted by one of the richest men in Italy. There is room on his jet for one more. I'd love it if you could join us."

I stared at her blankly.

Claire sat back in her chair, the smile suddenly leaving her face.

"You really don't know what I'm talking about, do you? My, how long have you been in Paris? What do you do here?"

I then spotted Dimitri and his client walking toward us. As she stood up to leave, Claire smiled in the direction of the fashion executive I was about to meet, who leaned over and kissed her on both cheeks, calling her by her French name.

"You know each other?" he asked, looking straight at me.

"We just met," Claire said. "I saw her sitting alone and came over to say hello. Lovely girl. I hope you do good things with her."

"We plan to," Dimitri said, ending the interlude. "And I must inform you," he said, a frisson of coldness entering his eyes, "that mademoiselle here is not one for you."

"Apologies for the lateness," said the fashion executive, who introduced himself as Thierry as Claire scuttled away. "Charmed to meet you. May I order you another drink?"

Forty-five minutes later, Thierry and Dimitri had ironed out details that were incomprehensible to me as I sat on my hands and chewed on my bottom lip. For my benefit, they spoke mostly in English, occasionally lapsing into French, talking about endorsements and residuals and commissions and cover shoots. I needn't really even have been there, although every so often Thierry would look my way, his cool blue eyes setting off his silvery hair. He had a perfect white smile, a few deep crevices in his forehead, and the longest fingers I had ever seen on a man. Apart from making sure he was pronouncing my name correctly, and asking me what it meant, he barely spoke to me. He squinted at my streak a few times, and then looked away again.

By the end of the evening, Dimitri and Thierry shook hands and promised that the paperwork would be signed in the morning. I, however, still had no idea what Dimitri had promised me to until a few days later, when Juliette brought home a copy of *Women's Wear Daily* and showed me a feature about Viva, its sale to Groupe Montaigne, and how it was poised to undergo a major revamp, including hiring a new spokesmodel for its next collection.

Three days later, a shiny black car came by the café to pick me up and to take me to a photography studio off rue Cambon. When I walked in, still in the *salwar kameez* I had worn to work that day, everybody stopped talking. A tall and extremely thin British man named Robert welcomed me, telling me he would be taking the pictures.

"Do you know what I'm doing?" I asked, realizing how stupid the question sounded.

"New international ad campaign for Viva," he said, stepping back and looking at me, as if through a camera lens. "You're their girl. Super exciting. Brand-new collection. The clothes are hot, finally," he added.

A blond woman with a friendly face guided me to a lit-up mirror in one corner, a tall chair set in front of it. From a large black suitcase she fished out dozens of eyeshadows and lip glosses, laying them out in front of me and asking me if I had any preferences. In the mirror, I saw Dimitri entering the studio and making his way toward me.

"Dimitri, I am grateful for what you have done, but I must make one thing clear," I blurted out before he even had the chance to say hello.

"You need to tell me what I am doing before I start doing it. I arrived here, and felt like a fool. I know that my career is in your hands, but I need to know what you are up to with me. I am sure I will agree to it, but you must tell me."

He nodded sheepishly.

"I didn't want you to concern yourself with these boring details. Just trust me. I am capable," he said.

"I am sure of that," I said as the blond woman applied foundation to my face with a wedge-shaped sponge. "But this is my life too. Let's be partners in it."

Compared to the exercise in humiliation I had undergone the previous week during my first real modeling job, this particular event was almost enjoyable. Everyone in the studio was uniquely focused on me, weighing in on whether my hair should be flatter or fuller, whether to go with the pink lipstick or the burgundy. Lights were moved around, music turned on so I could, Robert said, "get into the mood," and food was brought to me on pale green ceramic platters. When the time came for me to be photographed, I was told to stand on a large X-mark taped onto the floor, a sheath of thick white paper behind me. Robert told me where to look, where to put my hands, how much or little to smile, and I followed his instructions without thinking. He told me he could see that I was new to this but that I would pick it up in no time, and I felt reassured by that. He would only look frustrated when I lapsed into the habit—one that I thought all models had—of pouting like some coy Bollywood heroine about to be romanced for the first time.

"Stop that," he said when I did it for the fifth time. "Don't take this the wrong way, but you look like an idiot."

Even though Robert told me that he would have to take hundreds of pictures to find the perfect few that the company would use, I was still amazed at how long it took and how many outfits I was asked to change into. At one point, five people in the room were debating the merits of a particular belt, or would spend twenty minutes rearranging a cuff on my shirt. I couldn't imagine that the people who read the magazines these pictures would be used in would notice if a crease or a fold wasn't exactly where it should be. I did more poses than at one of my yoga classes back home—hands on hips, hands on butt, hands in air, legs crossed and then set apart, hair in ponytail one minute or spilling onto my shoulders the next. Even I, as accustomed as I was to the sight of me, didn't realize I had this many faces.

Five hours later, Robert announced that we were done. As his assistants packed everything away, he said he wanted to show me some Polaroids which, he explained, were always taken at the start of each session to make sure the lighting was right.

"In the end, I think this is the one they'll go with," he said. He lifted up a small square, showing me a photo of a girl I couldn't recognize. She was wearing skinny low-cut jeans that were held up by a thick belt covered in stones, and a sunshine yellow halter top. Her hair was combed completely straight and parted in the center. Large hoop earrings dangled from her ears, a thick ring studding her middle finger. She stood there, legs about a foot apart, her right thumb hooked through one of her belt loops. She looked like me, but older, sleeker, smarter—like in one of Nilu's magazines. She had, in her eyes, not even a hint of the fear of Allah preparing to destroy her. Her face betrayed none of the sadness of being made an orphan, and showed no sign of the loss of an entire life before this, an entire culture. As I stared at the sunny strength of the girl in the photo, I started to cry, knowing that I so much wanted to be her, but never could.

Robert, who had momentarily left my side to go check something with his assistant, turned around when he heard me sob.

"Gosh, they're not that bad, are they?" he asked, a look of genuine anxiety crossing his face.

"Oh no!" I said. "It's not that. They're very good. That's why I'm crying."

He looked at me, puzzled, and shook his head. I felt his hand rest on my lower back, and he turned to kiss me on the cheek, ignoring the tears that seemed to have collected by my earlobe. I felt his eyelashes flutter against my face, and it caused a tingle to run up and down my body. I drew in a sharp intake of breath, shocked at the newness of the sensation, and quickly moved away.

Chapter Fourteen

It took me a while to realize where the sound was coming from. For a few minutes I had been hearing an intermittent knocking from somewhere in the apartment. I listened some more, then heard my name being called. Softly at first and then a little louder.

"Tanaya! I'm here! Downstairs!" the voice said. I ran toward the window, peered into the street a couple of floors below, and saw Robert standing there, grinning up at me. Under one arm was a large flat, black case.

"I've been tossing pebbles at your window. Your buzzer thing down here doesn't appear to be working," he yelled up. "Just wanted to show you the final pictures from our shoot. I think you'll be pleased. Can I come up for a minute?"

I pressed the button to let him in and quickly dashed to the bathroom to rinse out my mouth; I had been eating tuna for lunch, straight out of the can, and our tiny living room and I both reeked of it. I grabbed a bottle of perfume from Teresa's closet and spritzed it into the air, waving away the bold, overflowery scent and causing the room to smell of jasmine and fish.

Robert was knocking on my door by the time I was done.

"Hello," he said. "Hope I've not come at a bad time. I was in the neighborhood, so thought I'd drop in, take a chance you were at home."

"Please, come in. May I bring you something to drink?"

"Coffee would be great if you have some. Sorry to just barge in like this, but I was so excited about these shots that I couldn't wait to show them to you. It's not something I usually do. But for you," he said, looking right at me, "I made an exception."

I excused myself for a minute to go into the kitchen and brew up a fresh pot of coffee, suddenly horrendously self-conscious—at the way I smelled, the way the apartment looked, at being alone with a man whom, I was now sure, was here for more than he let on. There was no reason I would know how to handle it.

Nervously I reentered the living room and sat on a chair across from Robert. He patted to the space on the couch next to him.

"It's OK. I can see from here," I said. He got up, walked around the table with his black case, and crouched next to me.

"No need to be nervous," he said quietly, putting his hand on my back again. "I'm not going to bite you, darling."

He opened his case and pulled out some large colorful photos: a carefree smile hovering on my lips, my hair tossed over one shoulder, my arms folded in front of me. I looked like I had been doing this for years.

"We had to do some retouching, just to even things out," he said, turning to look at me. "I mean, it's not like you're anything less than completely stunning." His eyes lingered on my mouth now. I stood up, telling him I needed to check on the coffee. He stood up too. Then he wrapped one strong arm around my waist and pulled me toward him.

"So tell me," he said in a grunting whisper. "That silver patch of yours up there, does it match the one down there?" His eyes lowered, and his hand started to move down my body. I grabbed it, holding it tight in my grasp. Then his mouth landed on mine, his tongue forcing my lips open. He smelled of cigarettes; his skin was coarse and rough. I felt a wave of nausea come over me, fear gripping my belly. I instantly had a flash of my mother and father on the night I was conceived, a miserable man pressing down on top of a desperate woman. I thought of those articles in *Teen Cosmo*, about how to attract the boy of your dreams and which lip glosses were most kissable, and I wondered why girls chased after something that was so obviously repulsive. As another surge of sickness overcame me, I pushed Robert away, ran back into the kitchen, and threw up in the sink.

"Please leave," I said, my voice starting to tremble.

"You've got nerve," he said. He bent over and picked up

his portfolio. "I thought you'd be a bit friendlier, given everything I could do for you."

I came out of the kitchen and looked at him.

"Well, my girl, I'm like *this* with the people at French *Vogue,*" he said, crossing two of his fingers in front of my face. "I could have landed you something pretty major there, something any other upstart model like you would do anything for. But you've just blown it, haven't you?"

He slammed the door behind him, and I started to cry.

"No matter how it might appear, that kind of behavior is not normal." Mathias looked over at me sympathetically as I took a break during my shift the next day. He had calmed down significantly since I first told him what had happened with Robert; his first reaction had been a desire to race over to what he described as "that British punk's studio," and, from the sounds of it, hit him.

"You know, people think that fashion is all about sex," he said, deep in thought. "I suppose in many ways it is. But then they think that all models are cheap, willing to give themselves over to anyone because, after all, they are willing to take off their clothes for a living. It's not fair, but it's the way this business is perceived. Perhaps the cad has never met a virgin model before."

I thought of Nana, who would grumble and groan each time he spotted a copy of *Stardust*—the glossy magazine charting the lives and loves of Bollywood's finest—in our house.

"Decent girls don't dress like this," he would spit out, pointing to the cover photo of a comely Aishwarya Rai in a belly-baring *choli,* her bountiful cleavage peeking through its sequin-encrusted surface.

I looked down at the snug jeans and T-shirt that Karla had insisted I wear that day and wondered what Nana would think if he saw me now.

The Viva ad campaign launched some weeks later. Dimitri showed me a couple of magazines and newspapers in which large ads were placed, a shiny, smiling me in full-color glory. My roommates, who had wasted no time in telling their other friends and colleagues that they lived with me, wanted to take me out to dinner to celebrate, to pop open a bottle of champagne and insist I take a sip — just one — to help me feel the thrill of this. For one evening they pleaded with me to forget that I was Muslim, and to succumb to the forbidden lure of alcohol. Instead, I kept my hand around a glass of club soda, sipping away quietly while they ordered another bottle of the bubbly liquor.

Chapter Fifteen

They had seen the photos, and Nana, so I was told, almost had a stroke. Aunt Mina, I had been informed by Shazia, had been sitting in the waiting room at the cancer specialist's clinic, had randomly picked up a magazine, and had to look five times at the picture before she realized it was me. The Viva girl was now in a light blue lace camisole and matching underwear, her head hanging upside down off a couch, hair sweeping a gold colored carpet, a round, ripe cherry in her red-painted mouth. Shazia said that her ailing mother had turned the magazine around countless times in a bid to rule out any possibility that it was me. But there I was, cleavage and all, my legs crossed at the ankle above me.

Owing to a newfound and curious affinity with my grandfather, Aunt Mina had ripped out the page and mailed it to him. After all, they both now shared the pain of having disobedient and disgraceful daughters. Such was their closeness, that my grandfather had even returned to the phone booth around the corner from our house to call Aunt Mina, to cry down the line about the shame of rearing a girl who had become, as he had put it, a "common prostitute." My mother had apparently snatched the magazine page from her father's trembling hand, ripping it into a thousand pieces, convincing herself that in so doing she was killing me off.

Why Shazia felt compelled to call me and tell me this I could not understand. It was like she wanted me to know that my family's disgust with me was now so profound and so complete, that I could surely never redeem myself with them, that any vague hope I might have had of reconciling with them in the future was now utterly trashed. It was like she wanted to ensure my isolation.

That night, smarting with shame, I lay in bed, willing myself to sleep and imagining Nana lying in his. He would do as he always did when bothered about something—stare at the dust-covered ceiling fan that whirred softly overhead, his hands folded behind his head, his glasses resting on the bedside table. He was probably praying that nobody else would ever see that photograph. I could imagine my mother in her own misery in the room next door, the room she once shared with me, mystified at how such a well-brought-up girl could have turned out so badly.

My last day at Café Crème came exactly three months and four days from when I had started there. After my first shoot with Viva, Mathias had reckoned that it would be just a matter of time before I would feel motivated to move on.

"There is no need for you to be sitting behind that desk and counting money when you are making so much of it on your own," he had said.

My contract with Viva was for a significant enough sum that I could have even moved out and rented my own place, probably somewhere hopelessly chic in the 16ᵉ *arrondisement*. But I was interested in no such thing. Karla, Teresa, and Juliette were still my only friends, and the only people with whom I spent time when I wasn't being photographed, strutting down a catwalk, or being filmed for a television ad. When Dimitri had arranged for me to be interviewed by *Madame Figaro*, one of the best-read publications in France, the reporter had used a headline that translated, roughly, as THE LONELY MUSLIM MODEL. She had asked me questions about my culture and faith, about how many times a day I prayed or whether I went to the mosque or if anyone in my extended family had ever considered being detonated. She asked me if I would eventually be one of numerous wives, consigned to living life in a burka behind the high white walls of a Saudi palace. I explained to her that I was Indian, and not Arab, that I ate no pork and consumed no alcohol but that being here, in Paris, I had figured out in which direction Mecca was and still prayed to it.

Then she asked me about my family, and how they felt about my newfound success, to which I mouthed a soft "OK. Fine."

"Actually, no, wait," I said to the interpreter. "That's not true."

I then told them about the scene in *Sabrina* that had pulled me toward this magical place, and the note with Tariq's phone number on it, and a cousin named Shazia who had been determined that I stay on here and to "follow my destiny." I told them about the grandfather I thought had loved me more than anything else in the world, and who now considered me dead, and a mother who didn't have the courage to fight for me. These were things I had told nobody, not even the girls I lived with, and while a part of me felt I was betraying the code of silence that is often imposed on girls like me, I didn't care anymore.

Shortly afterward, I stared at the printed article, a photograph of me atop a hotel roof, taken from the side, gazing over the buildings that crouched beneath. I looked as wistful and sad as I felt, the words conveying my melancholy. I carefully clipped the feature out, folded it neatly, and slid it into a large brown envelope. At the post office, I paid extra for special handling and delivery, a guarantee that it would arrive at its destination and that I'd be able to track it if it didn't. I sent it off and waited for the phone to ring.

Two weeks later, the envelope was returned to me, un-opened. On the front, I recognized my grandfather's hand-writing and the thin, dark-blue fountain-tip pen he always used, the ink spelling out the words: PLEASE RETURN. SENDER UNKNOWN.

Chapter Sixteen

Dimitri said he didn't want to lose me, that I was his best client, that my future was as bright as the moon and that I would be his nest egg.

But he said that to me as he handed over a plane ticket to New York. His eyes sincere, one palm pressed against his small face, he told me how much he would miss me, but that his cousin Stavros, who ran the New York branch of his operation, would look after me.

"Your future is there, not here. Of that I am sure," he said. "It's what the Viva people want. The campaign is global; the brand is booming. New York is the center of the world. When this contract finishes, there will be no end of opportunities, but you must be there to exploit them. Stavros will see to it. Don't worry about anything; from the time he picks you up at the airport, he will take care of everything. You will be to him like you have been to me, his number-one girl."

The girls threw me a farewell party, although only

Dimitri and Mathias were invited. We sat around the apartment and ate miniature quiches and vegetable terrine on crunchy toast, all courtesy of Café Crème. I drank apple juice while they had champagne, begging me again to have one little sip, just one, to properly bid them farewell. I shook my head, joking that I was in enough trouble with Allah to begin with, and they laughed as I cried.

Stavros was gorgeous. He had salt-and-pepper hair and pale gray eyes, and he was tall and tanned. He gallantly took my baggage cart from me as soon as he saw me, whisking me through the chaos of the terminal at JFK and into a waiting black car. Inside, he lit a cigarette, looked me up and down, and smiled through straight white teeth.

"You are going to have quite a career here," he said.

I turned to look out the window, trying to take in the roughness and speed of the city.

"So everyone keeps telling me," I said.

"Because it's true. Compared to Dimitri, I run a totally professional organization. I even have an office these days. I have some fabulous girls on my books, but nobody quite like you—nobody as exotic, delicate, and strong at the same time." He reached over and pulled aside my hair, which had fallen like a curtain over one side of my face. I caught the driver's eye in the mirror, and he averted his gaze, turning up the volume on the radio.

"Please, you're making me uncomfortable," I said,

moving over closer to the window. "I'm not accustomed to this kind of attention."

"Well," he said, shuffling back over to his side of the car. "Get used to it."

He had found me an apartment in a building with an elevator and a glass door in the front through which access could only be gained by pushing a code into a keypad. We were on the Upper West Side, a nice neighborhood, a place where I would be safe yet from where I could easily travel to shoots. He had put down two months' deposit on my behalf, which he would eventually deduct from my earnings. He handed over an envelope containing my schedule for the next day, five crisp hundred-dollar bills, and a subway card. Inside the small furnished apartment he had left a folder containing menus from nearby restaurants that delivered, along with a list of emergency contacts, his home and cell-phone numbers at the top. He told me to get some food brought in, to go to bed early, and that he would send a car for me in the morning. Then he shook my hand, stopped for a second to stare at me some more, and left.

I stood and looked around. There was a bedroom off the living room, the bed covered with an orange chenille blanket, a Chinese lantern shading a lightbulb on the ceiling. The attached bathroom was small, but done up in a pretty shade of lilac, and had been freshly cleaned, the smell of ammonia coming off the tiled floor. In the kitchen a cupboard held spices and cans of food, a partially filled fruit bowl rested atop a small corner table, and two large bottles of water took up part of the counter. There were stamps, extra keys, flashlights, a notepad. Stavros, it seemed, had thought of everything.

I wasn't sure what to do next, nor even what part of the apartment to venture into. It occurred to me that this was the very first time, in all my nineteen years, that I would be going to sleep under a roof where nobody else slept, that I would be completely alone, vulnerable to being attacked or killed. That somebody could break in, in the middle of the night, could rape and maim me, just like my grandfather had cursed. I closed the windows tight and made sure the door was locked. Then I called Shazia, comforted by the thought that she was only three hours behind me. I gave her my new number and made her promise to stay in touch. Then I retreated beneath the comfort of the chenille.

Madison, Fifth, and Park. Stavros told me that I needn't concern myself with any other parts of New York than those, with the exception of a party or two I might want to attend in an area he called the Meatpacking District, and which made me wrinkle up my nose at the vision of pork carcasses being hung up on large iron hooks, baffled that anyone would want to throw a party there.

But for now, I was going with him in a Town Car to meet someone from Pasha de Hautner, a famous fashion designer who was as wealthy as the women he dressed, and who might pick me to be one of his girls at his upcoming runway show.

"We have to shake things up a little," said Stavros, explaining his strategy. "Viva has been great for you, but we don't want you to be known for just one thing. The international catwalks are where all the action is, all the exposure. Pasha likes to select the models for his shows himself, especially the new ones. And those are the girls who eventually land on the cover of *Vogue*. We're overrun by Eastern European models at the moment—you know, those emaciated types who suddenly blossom once they land in New York. But you, Tanaya . . . you are something quite different."

Perhaps jet-lagged, perhaps still a little sad and confused, I didn't feel much like talking. It was if we were sitting in a huge parking lot that stretched across the city, the traffic barely moving. I had thought that only Mumbai had gridlock as bad as this. Even on the occasions I would accompany my grandfather from Mahim into the metropolitan areas, when he had had some banking or legal matters to take care of, I would always be amazed at the numbers of people crammed onto the streets, spilling out of buildings at lunchtime. Those were the only times I could see another India, the one that was new and modern, the tall buildings lined up along Nariman Point, barely any space between them, looking as if at any moment they might fall on top of one another. This was the place where black

Mercedes-Benzes were filled with young men in suits, talking urgently on their cell phones in the back while a uniformed driver carried them around the city to important meetings. This was the place where girls who had been born with looks, money, and slightly more permissive parents would stop for lunch at restaurants with names like Jazz by the Beach, dressed in colorful tops and tight jeans, sunglasses perched atop henna-dyed hair. I would gaze at them as I waited for Nana to finish whatever he had come into town for, and then he would take me by the arm and we would walk to Churchgate Station, my shoes getting stuck in the creviced roads, Nana taking care not to trip over a man heaving his torso around with handless arms. There, we would crowd into the second-class carriage, pressed into the thousands of workers who were making their way home from the business zone to the outskirts where they, like we, lived. If I was lucky, I would find a seat, and Nana would push me into it as he stood protectively in front of me. He would tell me to look at no one, talk to no one, to keep my eyes on the floor and a smile off my face. And when we arrived back at Mahim Station, covered with grime and sweat and soot, I longed to be back in the city, close to the perfumed girls and their handsome boyfriends.

New York, I decided, was like Mumbai, only cleaner. It didn't have the rainy-day prettiness of Paris, but the people could be as gruff. Everything felt rushed, as if time was slipping away and everyone had to eat, move, talk, and think faster than if they were anywhere else.

At Pasha de Hautner's office, it didn't appear that anyone ever ate. All the girls I encountered, from the receptionist who sat behind a glossy wood desk to the flurry of females who glided down the carpeted corridors, were mere slivers of womanhood.

Stavros had insisted I wear one of the Viva outfits that he had hung ceremoniously in my small closet, and I had selected a pair of rose pink corduroy pants, a chocolate brown jersey top, and a thick belt with a pink buckle. We sat on a beige suede couch to wait while one of the dozens of assistants who seemed to appear and vanish within seconds said she would let her boss, who was in another casting, know that we were here.

"Probably with one of those stick-thin Muscovites," Stavros said cynically. "Fashion needs curves again, which is why those girls should be out and you should be in," he said, casting an eye toward my bosom. "You are the young girl ingénue *and* the sophisticated woman. You have it all."

Forty minutes later, we were told that Pasha de Hautner was ready for us. We were led down a white-carpeted corridor and into a corner office that had full views of the city below, the people seventeen floors down looking like tiny alien creatures bobbing along the gray grid that crisscrossed the city.

"Don't get too close, might give you vertigo," said an unfamiliar voice behind me. I turned to look at the designer, who was staring straight at me, a slight smile lingering on the edges of a thin mouth. It was hard to tell how old he was; he could have been a tired forty or a young sixty or anywhere in between.

"Thanks for coming. Pasha de Hautner," he said, extending a hand before turning to give Stavros a kiss on each cheek.

"How was St. Bart's?" Stavros asked. "Nice tan."

"The island is always lovely, but it's just *all those people*," he replied. "Is there no place in the world that is safe from the tourist on the package deal? I thought St. Bart's would be the last refuge, but the bargain-hunter has managed to infiltrate that also. Of course, they're run out of town after a couple of days—can't bear the cost of a glass of wine with dinner—so I suspect eventually we'll have the place back to ourselves, thank heavens.

"So, what do we have here?" he said, turning his attention back to me.

"This is Tanaya Shah, new to the scene," Stavros replied. "She's lived in Paris before this, India before that. I thought she had a beautiful and exotic new look that might be perfect for your fall collection runway."

Pasha was ignoring Stavros and instead approached me directly. He gazed at me up and down, circling me as if I were a car in a showroom. When he stood behind me, I felt his eyes move from the nape of my neck down to my behind, and I was suddenly appreciative of the coverage that ultra-traditional Muslim women had on their bodies. At least they wouldn't have to contend with this gawking and mental undressing.

"Well, let's try her on for size, shall we?" he said to Stavros, a sly smile returning to his lips.

In another room, one of the girls handed over one of Pasha's creations, and I gasped at the beauty of it: fluid chiffon pants and a long tunic, covered with a heftily embroidered waistcoat, which the girl told me had been made in India. I lifted it up to my face, the wooden beads and sparkly sequins pressing into my skin, just to see if I could detect a scent of my country, perhaps a micro-drop of sweat from one of the workers who had toiled on it or a whiff of dust from the factory in which it was made. I held up the flowing, extravagant ensemble, and said to the girl, smiling: "Now *this* I can wear."

Pasha booked me for his next catwalk show based on seeing me in that outfit alone. But as a jubilant Stavros and I were about to leave Pasha's office, he whispered something into Stavros's ear. In the elevator, I pressed my agent to tell me what Pasha had said.

"He needs you to lose weight," Stavros said, eyes on the floor. "Ten pounds at least. Oh, and the gray hair thing? He thinks it's a gimmick; says it has to go, that you'll look too different from the other girls on the runway."

Chapter Seventeen

Stavros, I could tell, felt ashamed instructing me to lose weight, especially after his earlier speech to me, the one that celebrated my relatively curvaceous figure, at least compared to the reed-thin girls who he was convinced would hate me now.

"They will despise you because there are too many of them, and only one of you," he said. "You are their worst nightmare."

But while I had no real objection to losing weight, I put my foot down at Pasha's insistence that I cover over the pearly strands in my hair. I told Stavros to tell Pasha as much, and that if he was inclined to drop me from his show because of something that made me different, I didn't want to be part of it, not really believing the sudden strength of my convictions, but knowing that my Shah streak was far more important than a few minutes in the spotlight. I watched Stavros as he nervously dialed Pasha's number and spoke to him hurriedly, mentioning something about how the streak was my good luck charm. Then he nodded, smiled in my direction, and replaced the receiver.

"You win," he said. "But the weight still has to come off."

I had three weeks left until the start of New York Fashion Week, and while I had only been booked for one show, Stavros said this was going to be my New York debut, the one that would open the doors for me to fame, fortune, and endorsement deals.

"And you should start having some fun, too," he said. "What model has no fun?"

Almost as soon as Pasha had delivered his weight-loss directive, Stavros booked an appointment for me with a nutritionist who, in her sleek office on the Upper East Side, measured my body fat and wrote down everything I liked to eat: lentils and eggplant, chicken in butter sauce, and cardamom-infused rice.

"You don't actually have a weight problem," she said. "You're exactly where you need to be. Your caloric intake is a little on the high side, but your metabolism rate is high. In short, you can afford to eat," she said, smiling.

"It's in the genes," I replied, recalling the long, lean frames of my aunts, and their ability—like mine—to eat as they pleased without gaining an ounce.

"She's making her catwalk debut," Stavros interjected.

A frown appeared on the nutritionist's face.

"Ah, one of those again. Always happens this time of year. I don't like it, but I'll help you, if it's what you really want." She looked over at me again, a glimmer of disapproval in her bespectacled eyes.

"Start by giving up your morning *lassi,* and we'll go from there, OK?"

After stocking up on celery sticks and flax crackers, Stavros took me to meet with Marco, a personal trainer who had worked out with some of the best bodies in the business. He had close-cropped hair that reminded me of a military inductee, perfect bone structure, and muscles that bulged through a thin, light blue T-shirt. I felt self-conscious as he stared at me, asking me to stretch my arms out like a scarecrow, checking for muscle tone, telling me I didn't have much of it.

"You're not fat, and you have back fat. What's that about?" he asked, looking unimpressed.

"I've never exercised before," I said. "Well, maybe a little yoga with my grandfather. Does that count?"

He ignored me.

"Tomorrow, six a.m., we begin," he said, writing down my details on a clipboard.

I met him in Central Park. He showed me how to warm up, bending over to touch his toes. Meanwhile, I could barely reach my knees. He twisted his torso from side to side, grabbing me by the waist as I flinched, helping me to do the same. He strapped a little band onto my wrist that he explained would monitor my heart rate, then suggested I start walking slowly, increasing my pace as I went.

Everyone else around me looked as if they had been doing this all their lives, sprinting and talking with their running companions as they went, while I could barely go fifteen minutes without needing to stop and take a breath.

"Three weeks, girl," he said. "No time to be dragging your feet."

Afterward, he took me to a private gym where he worked me out on elaborate weight machines, laid me on the floor to do stomach crunches, and made me squat and rise repeatedly. Even in Mumbai's sultriest summers, with no air-conditioning in our home, I had never sweat this much. I couldn't believe that people actually enjoyed doing this.

In between all of this, and remembering to bake chicken and shred spinach leaves, I had to schedule fittings at Pasha's office. I was going to model four outfits, which had to be systematically taken in until the day of the show. Thankfully, I had no time to mope about being alone. And when I told Shazia, she was positively envious.

"What I wouldn't do to have someone care about every ounce I had on my wobbly behind," she sighed. "Tanaya, you don't know how lucky you are."

"Nine pounds, three ounces. Bravo!" Stavros said, peering down at the weighing scale in my bathroom. "You've done it!"

It was six a.m., and our call time was in a couple of hours. The show was one of the first of the day and, as

Stavros pointed out, because it was only the second day of Fashion Week, the style crowd hadn't yet developed the cynicism they were noted for, and thus it would be much easier to love a new and fresh face before the toll of the week had been taken.

I shrugged my newly slenderized body into a pair of jeans and a light sweater, and Stavros pulled out a pair of high heels for me to wear, telling me that I had to look like a model, even before the show. He was beginning to behave like the *ayah* I had when I was growing up, my pudgy Gopibhai, who fussed over me like I was a wounded bird.

Initially nobody backstage looked my way. We were at the Bryant Park tents, or "fashion central" as Stavros called it. Men with bright blond hair, buff arms, and high-pitched voices were fussing with curling irons. Women wore aprons around their T-shirt-and-cargo-pants-clad bodies, brandishing everything from fluffy makeup brushes to spritz bottles. Music coming from a sound system behind me was louder than it needed to have been, a string of rhymes and four-letter words rat-tat-tatting in my ears. The other models were immersed in their own world, reading glossy magazines or listening to their iPods or texting messages to some lover who might be awaiting them on the other side of the runway. Stavros was asked to leave and, telling me that I was in good hands, disappeared into the cavernous darkness of the long room I would soon be walking into.

All the commotion, combined with the smell of cigarette smoke that hung heavily in the room and the fact that I hadn't eaten in two days, made me feel lightheaded. I didn't belong here, and I would never be able to feign the coolness of these people.

"Hey, you're number ten," said a black man in a tight white T-shirt, streaks of orange running through his hair, as he glanced at a clipboard. "Let's get you situated."

He installed me in a chair and signaled to someone from the hair and makeup team to start working on me. One of the models in an adjacent chair finally took her eyes off her BlackBerry long enough to notice me.

"Hey, you're new aren't you?" she asked. "Haven't seen you around before."

"Yes, hello, my name is Tanaya."

"Pippi," she said. "Pleasure. Lovely name you have. Where's it from? I'm from London myself . . . Bolton, actually, but none of these other birds know where that is, so I just tell 'em London. Here. Fag?" she asked, offering me her packet of Winston Lights. I shook my head.

"So tell me, did that poofter Pasha by any chance tell you to drop some pounds? He does that to *all* the new girls. Sexual harassment, if you ask me. He's got some weird skin-and-bones fetish, I'm sure of it. But I live for this business, so I'm not one to speak, am I? Anyhow, losing the weight is easy. I'm sure you did what every girl in this business does, you know . . . the typical new-model diet?"

I looked at her, puzzled.

"Coffee, ciggies, and cocaine. Stick to that for a week, and even a mean old rump-humper like Pasha would be satisfied."

I had had a horrible migraine once, many years ago, and standing at the far end of the catwalk, preparing to walk down it, was a bit like that. The camera flashes went off with such ferocious intensity that, for a second, I couldn't see where I was going. I forgot where I was, what I was wearing, what had brought me here. All I could focus on were those hundreds of flashes, like exploding stars, right where I thought people would be. The numbness appeared much more quickly than in a migraine, starting at one side of my head and wending its way around and down the rest of my body. I was suddenly frozen. Under my breath, I whispered, "Nana," just like I used to when I would awaken from a bad dream and run into his room. The black man with the streaked orange hair yelled, "Go! Go!" from the sidelines. I put one foot in front of the other and walked, thrusting my hips from side to side, just the way I had rehearsed with Stavros. Somehow, and I don't know how, I made it to the end, thunderous applause elevating me and carrying me back the way I'd come.

It's true what they say about modeling: If you're any good at it, it feels like the most natural thing in the world.

I was, I realized after that terrifying flit down the runway, very good at it. By the time the second outfit was on and I was poised to make that journey again, it felt as natural as brushing my teeth.

Stavros, not one to idle away the hour-long wait before the show started, had decided to start a game of Chinese whispers. From his third-row seat, wedged between a fashion reporter for an online magazine and the owner of a boutique in SoHo, he told a story.

By the time the show was over, the story had reached the front row.

After it was all over, he returned with a bouquet of lilies, which he handed to me as I was unfurling the chignon I had been given. He reached down to kiss me lightly on the cheek. I was so buoyed, so suddenly and profoundly confident, that I wanted to turn toward him and let his lips touch mine. But I did not.

"You were magnificent," he said. "Everybody is wondering who you are."

Chapter Eighteen

Page Six of the *New York Post* is like the *paan* stall five buildings to the right of Ram Mahal.

There, Lakshman the *paanwalla* sits cross-legged atop a stained white cushion, passing on information about the neighborhood and its residents. If Mrs. Sharma from apartment 7-D had complained to him of chest pains that morning, then by noon Mr. Bhatia of the Soldiers' Colony down the road knew about it. If Ashok *seth*, the importer of towels who lived at Walia Apartments, was expecting a visit from the tax authorities next week, then Buntu, the young newspaper vendor across the street, would be happy to commiserate. Without having to leave his perch, Lakshman entertained and informed all those who stopped by his stall for a small green leaf stuffed with spiced betal nut.

The morning after the show, because of my photograph on Page Six of the *New York Post*, everyone knew me, even if what they thought they knew wasn't actually true. In the first place, I wasn't really an orphan. In the second, I had never been impoverished. Perhaps just the last word of the headline, FASHIONISTAS WOWED BY NEW MODEL — IMPOVERISHED MUSLIM ORPHAN OUTCAST, was correct.

Stavros swore to me that during his game of Chinese whispers, when he had told his seat neighbors to watch out for me, he hadn't told them that both my parents were dead.

"I might have intimated that they weren't around," he said. "You know how these things spread. And the impoverished bit: well, I think everyone just assumes that if you're from India, you're poor."

By the middle of that afternoon, Stavros had received six calls from other designers showing at Fashion Week, begging him to slot me into their shows, saying that they would create a spot for me even at this late stage.

"I could say yes, but I'm not going to," he said, smiling. "You're going to be the elusive one, the one everyone wants but nobody can have. That will be our power."

The girl that everyone wants. It felt unnatural to even think it, that a bunch of strangers, a group of fashion designers who had, until now, no correlation at all with my life would "want" me. My own mother hadn't wanted me. She had said as much to me a few days before I had left Mumbai, when my grandfather was asking me what I would be packing to wear to my "bride-viewing" meeting with Tariq.

"You must look nice and attractive," my mother had

said, barely lifting her eyes from the evening paper. "You must win him, and finally leave this house. Our burden will then become his."

My four turns on Pasha's catwalk led to lots of calls and offers, but there was only one that Stavros would accept: a four-page fashion spread in *Elle*—a feature showcasing fashion's current fascination with hand-embroidered tunics and flared silk pants. They were the kind of things Bollywood stars would wear when being photographed by *Stardust,* although in New York they cost a hundred times the price. I heard him on the phone with Dimitri, accepting congratulations for what was happening.

"We're aiming for the cover of *Vogue* and then a couple of big endorsement deals—I don't know, maybe Revlon or L'Oréal. Something global," Stavros said, his shirtsleeves rolled up, pacing around his office. "I know we're shooting high, but she's quite a commodity, this one. Best you've ever found. Don't worry, I'll reserve a few percentage points in my commission for you."

The morning of my shoot at *Elle,* which was set to take place in a penthouse apartment facing Central Park West, Stavros brought a woman named Felicia to breakfast. She had an oddly rectangular face, framed by masses of curly black hair, and a mouth that seemed slightly askew to her nose, like something out of a Picasso painting. But she had a nice, warm handshake and, compared to all the skinniness around me, had some flesh on her bones, a fact I found comforting. At last, here was someone unafraid to eat.

"Felicia's in PR," said Stavros, biting into a bagel. "She comes highly recommended. I just thought, with everything going on, we could use her expertise."

As she smeared jam onto a piece of whole-wheat toast, Felicia used words like "visibility" and "ubiquitous" and "mercurial." She told me that the marketing people at *Elle* were using today's shoot as part of a campaign, to expand past the "rich, white, and thin or brassy, bold, and black thing that fashion is all about.

"You represent a new demographic, a new era of multiculturalism," she said, noticing the confusion on my face.

"I'll break it down like this, honey. Being born Muslim was probably the best thing that ever happened to you."

Chapter Nineteen

Every budding fashion model, to ensure her success, needed to have some sort of social life. There were parties galore in New York, parties every night of the week, some in other glamorous cities. I was even being invited to one of the overseas ones, on a boat in St. Tropez the following month.

But in New York, Felicia handpicked the events I would go to, and would often escort me herself. There, she would deposit me with a Park Avenue socialite or a foreign aristocrat before surrendering her position as a shield between me and the paparazzi who attended these things. She told me delightedly that her job was made so much easier by the fact that I would never be seen with a cigarette or snorting cocaine or gulping from a bottle of beer, my panties exposed, a high-class hellion on heroin. She was relieved that no caption beneath a picture of me would ever say: HOT NEW MODEL TANAYA SHAH CAUGHT LAP-DANCING BAD-BOY ROCKER.

She dressed me in black halter tops and laced a shawl through my bent elbows. She taught me how to smile for the cameras, poised and pretty like the blue-blooded heiresses who graced the society pages. Whereas the small student-run newspaper in Paris that ran a grainy picture of me after my first little stint on the catwalk there had misspelled my name, now it was not only spelled correctly but typed in bold letters, as if suddenly, with four dress changes on a lit-up catwalk, I was no longer small and faded and gray, but dark, dramatic, and destined to be known.

Peering through the peephole, I could see that it was Stavros standing outside my door, a suit bag slung over his shoulder. Tightening my bathrobe, I opened the door and allowed him to step in. He took a look around at the immaculate room.

"Oh, the maid service has been here already?" he asked. "Didn't think they could be this efficient in St. Tropez during the height of the social season. My room is a mess."

"I did it," I said, glancing proudly at the perfectly made bed and the shiny coffee table.

Stavros stared at me, puzzled.

"You cleaned your own room? That's why people stay in hotels—so they *don't* have to do housework. They have maids here for that."

"Oh, I know *that*," I said, now embarrassed. I felt close

to Stavros, but still, there's no way I could have told him that, until today, I had never stayed in a hotel before, and that I thought that utilizing the services of the maid I had seen in the corridor earlier would cost extra. I had even brought my own towel, carried my own bag up to my room, and had had absolutely no idea what to do with the little card with the magnetic strip they had given me downstairs, having to wait until an employee passed by to open my door.

Later that evening, I waited nervously in the lobby for Stavros. A woman sitting across from me looked familiar, but I couldn't place her until she walked up to me, threw her arms around me, and gave me a hug.

"Tanaya, we met last year in Paris, at the Hôtel Costes. Remember? Claire?"

It suddenly came back to me. The Asian girl who wanted to befriend me and who Dimitri had later told me was a high-priced call girl.

"I've been in New York a lot recently, for business you know. I've seen you in the papers a few times. You sure have done well for yourself, although I'm not convinced about your goody-two-shoes thing." She sneered. "So, what brings you to St. Tropez?"

"The AIDS fundraiser," I said, adjusting the straps of my lemon-yellow chiffon gown, the one Pasha had made for me.

"Are you alone?" she asked, suddenly sweet. "I've been wanting to get into that event. Maybe I could come with?

As you can see, I'm dressed for it." She lifted up her hands and twirled around to show me her chocolate-colored gown covered with turquoise beads. For someone who had apparently no plans that evening, she certainly looked very nice.

"I was waiting around, you know, to see what turned up," she said, an enigmatic smile on her face. "There are lots of bigwigs in town for this event, and a few of them will be needing some company. I can come with you, and maybe we can hook up with someone afterwards?"

"My agent is taking me," I said, moving away. "I'm just waiting for him. So thank you, but no."

The gold doors of the elevator opened that minute, and Stavros appeared through them, looking more handsome than ever in a tuxedo. Claire's face lit up when she saw him.

"So *that's* your handler," she said, looking at him rather longingly. "Anyway, have a nice night, and maybe I'll run into you again sometime." She placed an icy kiss on my cheek.

A speedboat took us to a huge white yacht that sat serenely in the middle of the sea. It was a perfect night, cool and clear, like Mumbai right before monsoon season. Stavros held my hand and helped me off the boat and onto the floating palace, from where I could hear the sound of glasses clinking and piano keys tinkling and young women giggling. The yacht was owned by a software billionaire who had loaned it out to the charity for use that evening, and where guests had paid $5,000 each to dine on caviar and lobster medallions. Pasha, who had suddenly become my new best friend and had stopped talking about how pudgy I was, was hosting a table and had invited me, even paying for my airfare and hotel stay. Stavros insisted on coming along to chaperone me, for which I was immensely relieved.

"Ah, you made it. Welcome," Pasha said, kissing me on both cheeks. "The dress looks divine on you, darling. You do me so very proud. Now, quick smile for the boys," he said, twirling me around to face fourteen men with cameras. He placed me to his right at the table, a famous pop star he often dressed sat on his other side. Across from me was a rap artist who went by the name Baby Slut, and who was famous for the tiny, stublike dreadlocks pinched into his cropped hair and the sparkling sapphire embedded in one of his front teeth. He smiled at me as I sat down, the blue shine between his lips looking almost sinister. He put down his glass of champagne, heaved himself and all his gold accoutrements up from his seat, and came over, crouching down next to me.

"Hey, you the new model girl, yeah?" he asked, rubbing his pinky finger against mine, which I had read somewhere was known to be his particular mating call. "You look mighty fine. You wanna be my boo?"

Stavros, who was sitting next to me, diplomatically ushered Baby Slut back to his seat, turning my attention back to Pasha, who continued to pose congenially with me as the photographers circled the room. But as soon as the first course was being served and they were asked to leave, he stopped talking to me entirely.

"Sure I can't tempt you with a glass of wine?" Stavros joked, his shoulder rubbing against mine, the smell of vetiver coming off his freshly shaved skin. "Are you at least having a nice time?"

"Yes, but only because you're here." I smiled back at him, suddenly feeling warm and grateful.

An endless silent auction and three speeches later, everyone got back onto the speedboats to be taken across to dry land. As we disembarked, clouds began gathering overhead, and we heard the rumble of thunder in the distance. It was past midnight, and there wasn't a taxi in sight. The rain started coming down—a light sprinkling at first and then heavier drops. Stavros looked at me, helpless, trying to shield my head with his two hands as we raced back to the hotel on foot.

"Here," he said, spotting something lying on the street. He bent over and picked up a large black, empty trash bag and hoisted it above us, his two arms like tent poles. We ran back to the hotel, giggling. As soon as we arrived at the revolving-door entrance, we stopped, resting against the cool brick wall for an instant and dispensing with our makeshift cover.

"You OK?" Stavros asked gently, mopping my wet arms with his handkerchief.

"Fine," I said, staring at him, focusing on the droplets coming off his long eyelashes.

"That was quite an adventure," he said, laughing. He stared back at me, the smile slowly disappearing from his face. The night suddenly felt heavy with wetness, the rustling of leaves from nearby trees the only sound we could hear apart from our own breathing. Stavros leaned in, put one arm around my waist, and drew me to him, first lightly kissing my moist cheek and then smoothly moving his lips on top of mine. This time, I didn't flinch. I didn't fight. I simply let my lips relax under his and enjoyed the closeness.

After a few seconds, while my eyes were still closed, he stopped.

"I'm sorry," he mumbled. "I was overcome. It's been quite a night. Forgive me."

I nodded and said nothing. We silently went in through the revolving doors, me thinking about what I would say to him over croissants and coffee the next morning. Claire was sitting in the lobby, in the same place she had been hours earlier, but this time with a paunchy, well-dressed man, both of them swirling cognac in bulbous glasses. I knew she had seen me through the door because she smirked when we came in.

I was miss prissy-pants no more.

"You *kissed* him?! You frigging *kissed* him?!" Felicia screamed.

She was already waiting for me in the small lobby of my New York apartment building when I trudged in with my suitcase, looking as if she were about to explode. But she at least had the decency to wait until we were within the four walls of my apartment.

"What the crap were you thinking?!" she screamed again.

Felicia had received a call that morning from a tabloid editor with whom she was especially friendly. The editor had in turn received a call from one Claudine Chung, who had described herself as a Singaporean entrepreneur on business in the South of France who was willing to impart some scandalous information about me for a few hundred dollars.

"I thought I'd *never* have to worry about damage control with you!" Felicia shrieked. "But goddammit, of all the men to mess around with, you have to choose a married one!"

I dropped my suitcase.

"What? He didn't tell you?" Felicia asked, seeing the stunned look on my face. "OK, he's separated. But he's still married, for heaven's sake. To a hotel heiress at that. Do you know how that looks? A supposedly chaste celebrity smooching her married boss on a dark street in St. Tropez? What were you guys thinking? We're building your whole career on how fabulously elusive and traditional you are, and then you pull something like this!"

Felicia had talked the editor friend out of running any-thing, promising a much bigger scoop later on.

"Look, you're lonely. I get it," she said. "But that agent of yours is going to hear from me, I promise you that. In the meantime, let's figure something else out."

Stavros called soon after Felicia left. He apologized—first for kissing me, then for doing it while married. I had not seen him after that night, as he had chosen to stay on for an extra day, I assumed because he didn't want the awkwardness of being on a long flight with me.

"But why didn't you tell me you had a wife?" I asked him, feeling ashamed, reminding myself that infidelity was a severely punishable offense in Allah's eyes.

"Sometimes *I* forget that I'm married," he said sheep-ishly. "We've not been together in years and just haven't gotten around to getting divorced yet. But Felicia is right. That's no excuse. It was stupid and irresponsible of me, and could have easily destroyed everything we've worked for. Please forgive me. Can we forget it happened—put it down to a being-overcome-by-the-moment thing?"

I was prepared to do just that.

Felicia, in the meantime, had decided it was time to go on the offensive.

Chapter Twenty

"Here's the thing," Felicia said, her face turning serious, a cigarette dangling between two fingers. "I don't know how it is in your neck of the woods, but in these parts there's no such thing as a naïve, socially inept supermodel. It's an oxymoron. Understand?"

We were in her office, where she had hurriedly called a meeting with Stavros and me. On the way there, Stavros had described the event as a "summit," saying that Felicia could strategize more forcefully than an army general.

There in her office, Stavros looked at me, nodding in agreement.

"I've wanted to create a particular image for you — elegant, elusive, all that crap — and it's worked," she continued. "But it's just getting a little too stale, a little too vanilla."

"What do you have in mind?" Stavros asked.

"An alliance, quite simply," she replied. "An affair, but one that looks potentially serious, not some one-night-stand, roll-in-the-hay travesty. With a movie star or a rock star. All the girls have one: Gisele Bündchen's got Leo, Kate Moss has got that rocker chap, whatever his name is. We need to *align* you with someone who has a great profile, a strong image of his own, who can complement yours. Brad Pitt would have been perfect before Angelina pounced on him. Or Tom Cruise, but he's taken too, and anyway that Scientology thing wouldn't have meshed with your Muslimness, would it?" She snorted as I began to protest that "Muslimness" wasn't even a word. "But you know what I'm getting at. Right, honey?"

Nana, for all his steadfast traditionalism, would have understood. He believed that fortunes were built and families were founded on the basis of appropriate alliances. He might never have thought in terms of supermodels and rock stars, but he understood and agreed with the general concept. It still pained me to think of him, so I shut him out of my mind.

"Good point," Stavros interjected. "She needs a companion anyway. She can't be doing this circuit on her own for much longer. Even if it's a temporary thing, she must be seen to be somewhat *attached* to something other than a runway."

"I'm not really clear on what you're saying," I said, looking at both of them. "You can't just expect me to hook up with someone because he acts in movies or has a rock band. And really, I never thought I'd be with anyone until my wedding night," I said, blushing.

"Now that's just *adorable*," Felicia said. "But let me explain something to you. This supermodel thing, technically, is over. Sure, Victoria's Secret will always be there to make *someone* a star, but on their own, models are barely worth the clothes they walk in these days. It's all about brand-building, my girl. It's about endorsements and acting gigs and fitness videos and cookbooks and clothing lines and anything else you might want to do. If you're famous enough, people will eat at the restaurant you open and wear the bags you design and see the movies you act in. And how do you get famous? By being beautiful, which you are, and then hanging out with famous people, which you need to be doing more of. You need to be carousing on yachts in the Mediterranean with some A-list hottie, or be photographed in *Us Weekly* having a cozy coffee with whoever has the number-one single on *Billboard* that week. I told you from the beginning, this business is all about image. We need to cultivate a fabulous one for you, one that will take you to the top. Because that's where you are headed, child."

For a minute, it sounded like her speech was rehearsed, as if this is what she said to every ingénue who came through her doors. But I quickly realized that she must be talking to me, because I was probably the only nineteen-year-old fashion model she had ever met who needed professional help in finding a boyfriend.

Felicia spent the next ten days looking through copies of the *National Enquirer* and *In Style*. She called other publicists and her sister-in-law's best friend who worked at ICM in Los Angeles. She called a contact who freelanced for *Entertainment Weekly* and another who scouted male models for Calvin Klein. She compiled a list of prospects and, in my presence, started crossing them off one by one. The male models were a definite no, she explained to me, because they would be "too vain," and the competition between us would be too intense. There were some rising stars on the Hollywood scene who might be worth checking out, but the cross-country commute might be a bit too taxing, unless the prospect in question had the means to fly by private jet, and George Clooney had just come out of a relationship with a model. She thought aloud, reeling off names and facts and home addresses, as if any of it really mattered to me.

"Am I expected to do sex with them?" I said, ashamed at the question.

"You mean, *have* sex?" she asked, laughing. "Er, yeah. That's what an affair is primarily about."

I put my head in my hands. To Nana's dismay, I had yet to fully memorize the Koran. But I was certain that premarital sex was a sin. Even though, back in India, I only went to mosque once a week, walking along the plank of land that stretched into the Indian Ocean to get to the Haji Ali that lay at the end, and even though I was certain that there were plenty of Muslim girls everywhere who contravened that particular edict, I was not about to be one of them. I had done enough to disgrace my nana already.

"I'm sorry, Felicia, but I can't. I don't see myself lying between sheets, naked, with some white-skinned boy. I don't want to be touched by anyone until we have been blessed by a mullah and my grandfather has blessed me with his hands on my head . . . ," I said, my voice trailing off as I realized that would never happen anyway. I started to cry.

Felicia stopped her strategizing, sat back in her chair, sighed, and closed her eyes.

"Don't worry, Tanaya," she said, reaching a sympathetic hand across her desk toward me. "We'll think of something."

His name was Kai. There was no last name, not even an initial. Just Kai. He had opened for Coldplay and Maroon 5 six months ago, and now a single from his just-released album had gone multiplatinum. He was British, from Birmingham, and had conquered the United Kingdom before alighting in the United States. "He's the personification of Brit pop," Felicia said excitedly. "It's no longer underground, and it's all the rage, and kids like Kai are making it big." He was, Felicia continued to point out to me, "absolutely the hottest thing in music today. And cute, too."

She had come over to my apartment on a Saturday afternoon as I was packing to leave for a magazine shoot on the sandy beaches of Jamaica. From her bag, she took out a folder containing press clippings and photographs of the man that I was, apparently, going to embark on my first fully fledged romantic relationship with—fake or otherwise.

He had been chosen as one of *People* magazine's 50 Most Beautiful People, and I had to agree with them. In the clipping she showed me, his hair was dark like mine, spiked up in the front with a smidgen of gel. He had a happy face, slightly creased around the eyes, a shadow of stubble around his mouth. He was swinging from a hammock, his hands folded behind his head, a yellow-colored shirt open to halfway down his chest, a guitar resting by his side.

"I'm telling you, he's the one," she said excitedly. "I came up with a reasonable excuse—something about maybe you and him getting together on his next music video. You know, to wear something sexy and dance in it. We can work all those details out," she continued, waving her hand dismissively.

"Oh, and don't worry about it," she went on, watching a look of dismay cross my face. "You won't have to stop being a good Muslim girl. The boy is gay."

As fate would have it, Kai's people told my people that he could drop in on my magazine shoot in Jamaica. He was, I was told, currently casting for his next few music videos and was aiming to have one of them nominated for the MTV Music Awards, so he was going all out to find the best director, best choreographer, and sexiest story line. I was no stranger to him, apparently. He had seen a ten-second clip of me on the red carpet at a movie premiere in

New York I had attended recently, and told his people who told my people that I had looked "intriguing." So he was flattered, if not a little surprised, because, as his manager told mine, Kai didn't think I would be interested in "that kind of thing."

Once it had been decided that Kai would meet me in Jamaica the day after I got there, Felicia and Stavros booked themselves on flights as well.

"We gotta huddle," Felicia said as we waited at the check-in counter at JFK. "This needs to be planned perfectly. Can't let you negotiate this on your own."

Stavros, clutching his passport and the ticket that I knew was coming out of my paycheck, looked at me sympathetically.

Jamaica was unbearably hot. There was no way anyone could walk on the sand without sneakers on; even rubber flip-flops looked like they might melt under the strength of the sun. The water was sparkling and clear, and palm trees swayed at one end of the long beach.

In India, they would have had a sedan chair for me, a seat on two long wooden poles to carry me from the hair-and-makeup cabana to the water's edge, where the photography was happening. But instead, two men, employees of the hotel where we were staying that owned this particular stretch of beach, hoisted me up and carried me along, setting me down where the cool, salty water softened the sand and tempered the blazing heat.

I was wearing a gold bathing suit, my hair tight and uncomfortable in cornrows. The theme of the magazine spread was "the sexiest swimsuits in movie history," so I was being made to look like Bo Derek in *10,* right before she meets Dudley Moore. Next up was Raquel Welch's fur bikini.

The men who had carried me picked me up again, about to plop me down a few feet farther into the water, listening carefully to the instructions of the photographer, when I heard Felicia, who was wearing a hat the size of an umbrella, yelling to me from beside the cabana.

"He's here!" she screamed out excitedly. "I see the posse approaching!"

I looked up and saw the man who was number twenty-eight on *People*'s list of gorgeous people, and decided that Kai should have been closer to the top. He emerged from a walkway that led from the hotel down to the beach, clad in a loud red shirt emblazoned with Gothic crosses, his hands plunged into the pockets of his denim jeans, large sunglasses covering the top half of his face. Even with all the cameras and equipment and chaos on this mild beach, he stood out like a boil. His "posse" was actually only three people, one of whom, based on sheer size alone, had to have been his bodyguard. Kai looked over in my direction and I realized to my utter horror that I still had two uniformed hotel employees holding me up, a leg each, with me squatting between them. I could only imagine how ridiculous I looked.

Kai grinned in my direction, waved, and continued to

saunter my way, Felicia now affixing herself to his capsule entourage. The photographer rolled his eyes and told everyone to "take five." We were all officially on a break.

"Good to meet you," Kai said, extending his hand, which was soft and white in mine. His dark hair was nonchalantly swept back, revealing immaculate eyebrows, of which I was suddenly jealous.

"Do you want to go somewhere to talk?" he asked, smirking at the sight of me being held aloft by two men. "Not now, whenever you're done. Don't want to interrupt the work you're doing here."

I blushed, embarrassed, and Felicia led him away, whispering in his ear.

Before Kai and his group were set to join us, Felicia, Stavros, and I did our "huddle" in the restaurant, which was essentially one huge, open veranda overlooking the beach and the shimmering sea beyond it. Now, just after sunset, the air had cooled and a fresh breeze blew in from over the ocean. Diners reclined on daybeds overflowing with cushions, low tables in front of them holding large platters of freshly caught fish grilled with lemon and crisp salads drizzled with aged balsamic.

"You like, no?" Felicia asked, lighting up a cigarette. "He's a hottie. What'd I tell ya?"

That night, after dinner, during which our respective camps would discuss a nonexistent project between us, I should suggest that Kai take me for a walk on the grounds, Felicia said.

"That'll give me and his people a chance to talk," she said, eyeing a tray of rum-laced cocktails as it went by. "We may as well come out with it."

Nana, had he still been a witness to my life, would have been impressed by this. This was, after all, *exactly* how things would have been done had I remained in India and agreed to wed. He would have summoned some prospects, his friend's grandson Tariq being on the top of the list, and then casually suggested after dinner that the boy and I take a walk around the building. By the time the boy and I would have returned from the walk, we would be engaged.

To me, sitting there in a gauzy poncho and sequined sarong at a five-star resort hotel on the Jamaican bay, that all seemed like a lifetime ago.

Chapter Twenty-one

We flew back to New York together on Kai's private plane.

He sat across from me in a caramel-colored seat, his slender frame almost dwarfed by its depth and plushness. He had one leg crossed over the other, and his left hand cupped his chin. He had been staring at me for at least five minutes, all the way through our take-off, as I nervously tried to drink a glass of iced tea. If I didn't know any better, I'd think he was in love with me.

"Want to try one of these?" he asked, holding up a can of Red Bull, something he said he drank several times a day.

"Thank you, no," I said, shaking my head. "I'm happy with what I have."

"So, you know what all this is about, right?" he asked. "You know what we're doing here?"

I nodded.

"I know why *I'm* doing it," I said. "But what do you get out of it?"

"Please, don't tell me you haven't figured it out," he replied, rolling his eyes. "I'm supposedly the hottest thing in music since the Beatles, and I've never had a proper girl-friend. My agent had to remind me that rock and sex go pretty much hand-in-hand, and that without gossip about groupies, I may as well throw it all in and become a book-keeper. I've had a few beards over the past couple of years — you know, female friends I call on to hit the clubs with, get my picture taken. It keeps my gayness at bay, as far as my fans are concerned. But my team thought it was time for something a bit more established. Or at least they thought it once your people proposed it after dinner last night. You know, it's not a bad idea. I have a record coming out soon, and if I want to continue living like this," he said, indicating the plane, "then I'm going to need all the help I can get. You're a great wagon to hitch my ride to."

I suddenly felt soiled, as if I had allowed Felicia to talk me into something that was, fundamentally, unethical. Felicia's words about this whole business being built on image still smoldered in my ears. But now, agreeing to this sham of a relationship, I was giving in to it. Now I really was going to be lost in the celebrity shuffle.

But it was too late to do anything about it. Before Kai and I boarded the flight earlier that day, we both signed documents stipulating the terms of our relationship. There

were confidentiality clauses and endless paragraphs devoted to financial details. I was amazed at how the people
who worked with us managed to get it all together—legalese
intact—less than twelve hours after first discussing it.

I hadn't fully read all of the small print, quite happy to
take Felicia's word for it that everything was in order. I
had skimmed over the section that outlined how we would
both respond to queries from magazine editors and talk-
show hosts about how we met, and if we were in love, and
where the relationship was headed. We were to be seen a
certain number of times together every week, the exact
nature of which meetings were to be determined by us,
but would definitely have to include awards shows or
nightclub openings. We had to be photographed kissing
wherever and whenever possible. We had to have the
appearance of living together, even if we both maintained
our own apartments. And we had to keep it going no less
than a year, at which time we could release a statement
saying we had split amicably. By then, both our careers
would be soaring.

If my nana hadn't died of shock by now, this would definitely do it.

Our plane landed on a private airstrip just outside New
York. As the stairs lowered, Kai grabbed his bag with one
hand, and took my hand in the other. He had put on a pair
of dark glasses, pulled out his shirt from his pants, removed his socks. He looked scruffy, relaxed, sexy. He sug-

gested I leave my sunglasses off, that they needed to get a really good look at my face, and I agreed.

As we descended the stairs, I noticed that the airstrip was completely bare, except for a car that was there to pick us up. And then, popping out from behind a van like a gopher, I spotted a photographer, a camera slung around his neck, a cell phone attached to his belt loop. He smiled, took the picture, gave us a thumbs-up, and drove off.

Felicia, as always, knew just who to call. We were the lead item on Page Six the next morning, on the inside page of *USA Today*, and on seven different Internet gossip sites.

MUSLIM SUPERMODEL FINALLY HOOKS UP! screamed one headline.

ROCK DUDE SWEEPS AWAY FASHION'S LATEST HOTTIE! said another.

KAI AND TANAYA: FORBIDDEN LOVE? speculated an online column.

At my apartment, alone, I slammed shut my laptop, set the newspapers aside, and took the phone off the hook. I went into my bedroom and opened the top drawer in my bedside table. I rummaged around for something that Stavros had given me not long after I got here. I finally found it, held it tight in the palm of my hand, and went back outside to the living room.

Staring at the compass, I located the direction that, thousands of miles away across oceans, lay Mecca, our big, glorious, historic place of worship. Then, for the first time in months, I lowered myself to the ground, closed my eyes, and prayed.

Shazia, an avid reader of all things gossipy, was on the phone in no time. She was always fascinated by where I had gone the previous night, whom I'd had lunch with, what I was wearing, which country I was traveling to next. She had asked me to lobby Stavros to find me something in Los Angeles. She said she really missed me and wanted to see me again, but I think she wanted me around so she could latch on to the vague aura of stardom that seemed to have enveloped me.

"*Kai* . . . you're going out with *Kai?*" she asked, sounding more excited about it than I was. "He's so yummy! How'd you score that? Come on, seriously, tell me. Oh, and what's he like in the sack? I'm *dying* to know. I told the girls at work I'd find out from you."

"How's your mother?" I asked, sidelining her questions completely. "And have you been back to Paris recently? I'll be going, in a couple of months, for couture. You should meet me there," I said, wishing immediately that I could have taken the words back.

"Oooh, I'd love it!" she squealed. "Will you get me a front-row seat? Can I come to the parties with you? Will there be gift bags? Oh my God, will Kai be there?"

I realized then that the only thing worse than being a groupie, was having one in the family.

As my "relationship" was proceeding as planned, it wasn't too hard to stick to the terms of our agreement. By this point, Kai and I had repeated our story so many times, it had become rote. And yet we somehow both managed to sound as excited, as if it were all true. It was a story shrouded in glamour, enfolded in allure. I was on a magazine shoot in Jamaica; he was there on vacation. He had vaguely known who I was. He saw me as I emerged from the pool and watched stealthily as I wrapped myself in a pareo. He sent over a cocktail, and I turned it down because I didn't drink. He was charmed, he said, and hooked. He played his guitar to me as we sat on a rock by the beach, under the moonlight. He sang of lost love and dashed desires, his number-one song that summer. The chemistry was unforgettable, he told everyone. By the time he was done telling the story, me blushing at his side, even I believed him.

The voice on the phone was faint at first, vaguely recognizable. She repeated my name over and over, as I stopped breathing, wondering if it could really be . . .

"Nilu?" I said. "Is that you?"

"Yes! Tanaya!" She sounded thrilled. "I'm in New York. I *had* to look you up."

Getting my number was a long and arduous process, apparently—beginning with calling the switchboard at Blaze, a makeup line with whom I had just signed an endorsement deal. Five different connections later, she had reached Stavros, who recognized her name from my stories and had immediately passed on my number. I stood in my apartment, the phone to my ear, trembling, delighted to hear the voice of someone who knew me before all this started.

She was only in town for a few days, so we made plans to meet immediately. Her brother, a systems analyst in London, had come to New York for a job interview and had asked his sister to join him for a few days. He was making enough money to get her a visa and buy her a plane ticket, so she didn't hesitate.

We met outside a restaurant in Greenwich Village, close to the apartment she was staying in with her brother and a friend of his. I saw her approaching, turning a corner at the far end of the street, and I ran toward her, my heels clicking along the pavement. I stood in front of her, saw my ecstatic face in those small round glasses of hers, and flung my arms around her.

"I can't tell you how happy I am to see you," I whispered in her ear, trying to stifle my tears. "I can't tell you what it's been like not to have my friend."

She hugged me back, tightly.

"I'm here now, Tanaya!" she said, brightly. "For a few days, anyway; it will be like old times."

I couldn't even wait for the menus to arrive before barraging her with questions—about Mahim and Mumbai and the weather and the latest movies. She told me that I had been the subject of a recent profile in the *Times of India*, a generally positive feature about a Mumbai Muslim who had made it big in the world of modeling.

"On our street, everyone is so proud of you," she said, breaking off a piece of bread and wiping the crumbs away on her napkin. "The *paanwalla* tells me everything, that people stop by and complain about the economy and the rain, but always say, 'Hah, but that pretty Shah girl from Ram Mahal, now she is doing *very vell.*'" I laughed at Nilu's rendition, but could imagine the chatter on the street, the claims to fame at the corner stall.

"Really," Nilu said, now serious. "You've done something great, Tanaya. You know, I am now at Mrs. Mehra's School of Domestics? Where else would I go? But you have escaped all that. You are doing what I knew you always could. You are making your own money and creating your own name, no more just Zakir Shah's beautiful granddaughter from flat 1B. Do not be ashamed," she said. "Be proud. I am very proud of you."

I was quiet for a moment, waiting for her to answer a question I couldn't ask.

"Yes, I saw them," she said softly. "I went by there when I knew I was coming here, to try and maybe get your contact details. I had thought, possibly, that you wouldn't be on speaking terms but wasn't sure, that maybe Nana wasn't as stern as you made him out to be. But, after I saw him, I guess I could see why you were always afraid of him."

I chewed on my straw, scared for her to go on, but needing to hear about my family from someone who had just seen them. I had been gone almost a year, my new life unrecognizable. Some of the other models I had be-friended here rarely spoke of their families, and if they did, it was usually as an afterthought. Until the day I got on that plane for Paris, in search of Sabrina, my family had been my entire existence.

"Well, it will just hurt you to hear it," Nilu said, as she looked at my questioning face. "We should talk about other things. Your life is beautiful now. There is no need to put yourself through this."

"No," I said, placing my hand on top of hers. "Just tell me how they are, Nana and my mother. How they look. How their health is. What they said . . . ," I stammered, "when you mentioned my name."

She looked down at her food for a minute, unsure.

"Your grandfather has always been very nice to me," she said. "Every time I came over to see you, he would al-ways go down to the corner and buy candy for us to share. Remember? And anytime there was a new *Archie* comic at the bookstall, he would bring it for us to read together." Her face softened into a smile as she thought back.

"But when I went over there last week, as soon as he opened the door to me, his face turned so gray and angry, I swear I thought he was going to slap me then and there," she said, the smile disappearing. "For a minute, I think he thought that it was all my fault."

I felt the tears returning, but wiped them away. People in the restaurant had already recognized me, and I could already anticipate the headlines: SUPERMODEL BREAKS DOWN OVER LUNCH WITH MYSTERY WOMAN. My life, I could see, had become a series of newspaper captions.

"You know all this already, Tanaya. Don't make me go on," she said. "It's as painful for me to tell it as it is for you to hear it."

"I need to hear it anyway," I said. "If that is the only thing that helps to keep my nana and mamma in my mind, then it is better than nothing."

She sighed and stabbed her fork into some slivers of beet.

"He wasn't happy to see me, but he invited me in anyway," Nilu continued. "He's always been very polite that way, no? Your mother was there, in her room, and she came out when she heard my voice, but didn't say anything. Your servant offered me tea and biscuits, but I said no. We just stood there, the three of us, in the little corridor. I asked how they were, and they nodded but said nothing. Then Nana asked me what I wanted, and I said I was there to see if maybe he had your phone number in New York. He looked shocked. Tanaya, do they even know what part of the world you are living in?"

I felt ashamed suddenly, that I was now not so different from the other girls I had met here, the ones from Missouri and California and Alabama who had to forsake their families and their former lives for fame and free martinis in

New York. I had never wanted to be one of those girls. But now, with my closest relatives not even knowing where I was, I had become one. It was apparent then that either Aunt Mina had stopped communicating with my grandfather or Shazia had finally stopped talking to her mother about me. The dusty web of family relations that my grandfather had tried so hard to keep intact no longer included me.

Chapter Twenty-two

To me, confidentiality agreements didn't apply to best friends. While the law might have stated otherwise, there was no way I could allow my best friend from home to think that I was actually dating a bad-boy rocker with a baby face and a tattoo that stretched from his elbow to his shoulder. Looking at Nilu's face, I could tell that she didn't believe it anyway, which was the fundamental benefit of having a friend who really knew you.

"Saif was still sending me magazines," Nilu said, giggling as we left the restaurant and walked down the street toward where she was staying. She had her arm looped inside mine, the way we always walked back on the streets of Mahim. "I have read all about your love affair. He seems nice," she said. "But I never would have pictured you with someone like that. I had thought, that even with all this, your glamorous life and all, that you might still want to wait. You know, until you found 'the one'—someone who loves Allah like you do, someone your family would approve of. But I guess it's hard, living here amidst all this, not to become a different person. He's rich and good-looking and famous, and so are you. So what does it matter?"

I could tell that Nilu was trying hard to keep the judgment out of her voice. She had always been kind and tactful, and I somehow always imagined her working as a diplomat. Unlike Nana, she would never impose her beliefs on anyone.

"I'm not supposed to tell you this, but it's not what you think," I said, stopping, the warm air from a sidewalk grate sweeping up our skirts. "This whole thing with Kai, nothing is really happening there, no matter how it looks."

She stood with her mouth slightly agape, her eyes wide behind her glasses, and listened as I told her about Felicia's plan and Jamaica and the chasteness of my relationship with a rock star.

"We have kissed for the cameras, but that is all," I said. "If we think a photographer has followed us, he will come to my apartment, then leave after drinking a cup of hot chocolate. People call our affair 'sultry' and 'hot' and God knows what else, but there is no such thing. In fact, it is really rather tame. We are like brother and sister. But I signed a piece of paper that said I could never tell a soul about this. So you must *promise* me that it goes no further. It doesn't matter what people say about me, if, when you go home, they call me a whore and a hussy. You *must* be absolutely quiet about this, believing the same as them. Maybe one day, far in the future, the truth can come out. Just not now. OK?"

"Why are you doing this?" she asked. We continued walking, Nilu squeezing my hand, a light drizzle that had suddenly appeared merging with the tears on my face. "What purpose does it serve to have people think something about you that isn't true?"

"You know, Nana never thought I was worth very much," I said, my head bowed in sadness. "He thought that all I was good for was this face, that it would be the only thing to land me a rich and fine husband. But as it has turned out, my career—this thing I do—it's all I have now. I have to make the most of it. It is my intention to be as successful as possible in a very short span of time, to earn and save as much as I can. And then I will take what I've made and do something significant with it, although I don't know what yet. Maybe, in the end, it will help me to win my family back. Although maybe by then, also, the damage will have been too much. But the people who work with me, the people I trust, they have told me that if I do this, I will go from being a fairly famous fashion model to an extremely famous one."

Nilu nodded, then was silent for a minute. "Tell me something," she asked as we arrived at the entrance to her building. "After everything you've been through, do you think you would do it again, leaving India and all? With all that you've lost, I mean with your family and all, has it been worth it?"

I gave her a hug good-bye and, just as she was pulling away, whispered into her ear: "Yes."

Chapter Twenty-three

For someone who had never had to manage money before, I had become rather good at it. I used to live on a weekly stipend—about the equivalent of five dollars—which would have bought me a coffee and a bagel on the streets of New York, but in Mahim allowed me to indulge in several movies a week from Book Nook, daily *dosas* at the neighborhood *dhaba,* and my monthly issues of *Stardust* and *Cine Blitz*, even if they were used. Occasionally I was able to save a few rupees at the end of the week, and when I had left for Paris, in addition to the small amount of money Nana had given me, this was what I had taken. It was a beautifully uncomplicated life. Money, for all I could care, was something to be spent on cold coffee and cotton candy. Before all this had happened, I figured that I would eventually be married someday, and to a man who would give me an allowance in order to purchase vegetables at the market and pay the *dhobi* to wash our clothes.

Stavros had helped me open a bank account shortly after I came to New York and helped me invest the money I had made in Paris. In addition to being my agent, he also called himself my manager, tending to what he described as my "business affairs." The payments for everything I did, from the runway shows to the magazine shoots to the advertising campaigns to the makeup endorsement deals, would initially go to him. He would deduct his commission and then send me the rest. I had no cause to question the way he was doing things. Every so often, he would sit me down and tell me all the expenses that had to be paid—Felicia's salary, my rent, cash for my personal expenses. He aimed, as much as possible, to ensure that I got as much as I could without paying for it: my clothes from Viva, for whom I still worked, more out of a sense of loyalty than anything else; my makeup from Blaze; and just about anything else I wanted by calling a stylist. He educated me about the power of demands, how I could use as leverage my growing fame, and that designers would fall over themselves getting me in one of their outfits if they thought it would result in more business for them. I eventually understood how this world worked, although I never felt comfortable just assuming that things were there for me, just for the asking. It was interesting that while Nana believed in hard work, and had had the same job as an airline pilot for more than two decades, he had never inculcated that in me. He had taught me the importance of saving money. But earning it, as far as he was concerned, was not something I ever had to worry about.

So just short of a year from the time I left India, now officially out of my teens, I was stunned to see the amount of money in my savings passbook. I took out a calculator and worked out what it was in rupees, then determined that in all the twenty-three years that my Nana worked as a pilot, he never made what I had accrued in twelve months. But I knew he would be as impressed by that as if I had told him that I had made the money selling my body as a prostitute. To him, it would all be the same thing.

"How about Parrot Cay? Turks and Caicos?" Kai asked me one afternoon as he lounged on the couch in my living room, scraping something out of his right ear. I smiled as I thought of how this was the same man, with his toenail infection and the retainer he put on every night before bed, that millions of girls all over the world lusted over. They bought T-shirts with the words MRS. KAI scrawled over the front, and had his face as their computer screensaver. They would envy me for everything I knew about him; for a fake relationship, we spent a lot of time together, perhaps because our profile made it hard for him to be seen with anybody else. In a sense, he was almost stuck with me.

"Huh?" I asked, rearranging the kitchen cabinets.

"To vacation in. Turks and Caicos Island, at the Parrot Cay Hotel over there. Don't tell me you haven't heard of it," he said, noticing the blank look on my face. "Oh girl, where have you been? It's where Ben Affleck and Jennifer Garner just got hitched, where Bruce Willis has a pad. It's the vacation spot of the moment. It'll be great for us to be seen there. Anyway, don't you need a little break from all your shoots and shows and stuff? I know I do."

"What, just the two of us?" I asked. "Why do we need to go away together? You can have a break here, sleep in late, don't take on as many gigs." I wanted suddenly to start quoting the terms of our contract to him, to point out that nowhere was anything written about romantic excursions.

"Well, I really want to go, and I obviously can't be seen alone, because then the buzz will be that we've split up and all those gay rumors will start flying about again. So if I want to go, you don't really have a choice but to come with me."

I didn't even bother packing, simply pulling out from under my bed the slim silver gray Samsonite I had just returned with after three days in Bermuda for *Sports Illustrated*. I was certain that everything I needed was in there: swimsuit with the appropriate cover-up, sandals, floppy hat, suntan lotion. In India, I had been to the beach exactly three times, the last being when Nana had taken me horseback riding when I was thirteen. I had fallen off the horse, my foot entangled in the reins, and it had dragged me along, my hair sweeping the sand, the animal's warm, furry body flexing against my ears as it cantered along the water's edge. I emerged shaken but safe, and Nana had said he would never again take me back, that beaches were bad luck for me. Ironically, these days, I felt like I was spending almost all my life on them.

I was hoping Felicia would find some excuse to tag along, but even she—who could always somehow dream up reasons to treat herself to a first-class airline ticket on me—couldn't justify this.

"I have to say, I don't know why he wants to take you off alone. It's not like there's some major event or film festival happening there," she said. "Maybe he just wants to be alone with you. Maybe he's, you know, *changed*, and is falling for you. Would you even know how to recognize the signs, you virgin you?"

"Don't be ridiculous, Felicia," I said, fiddling with the locks on my suitcase. "I think he just really wants to go, and could use the company. Just thought you might want to come along, but of course he doesn't know that I'm asking you."

"Sorry, my dear. It will look really odd; you, your alleged boyfriend, and your publicist, all on vacation together. But don't worry. I hear from his old boyfriend that he's romantic and attentive," she said, laughing. "Maybe he just wants to love you up. Enjoy! And if nothing else, you'll get a decent tan out of it. Oh, and hit him up for some beauty secrets. His skin always looks so great."

Kai chartered a plane to take us from New York to Providenciales, the main island in Turks and Caicos. Even though I hadn't been that keen about coming, I had to concede that the place was stunning. A water taxi took us from the airport on the forty-five-minute journey to Parrot Cay, which, from afar, looked unassuming, reminding me

fleetingly of a Hyderabadi bungalow. But what was striking was the splendid blue-green of the sea and the blinding
whiteness of the sand. There seemed something uniquely
untouched about the place, and I began to relax and lose
my resentment at being brought here, now looking forward to a few days of nothing to do but read the Harlequin
novels I'd thrown in my bag, and listen to old Hindu clas-
sics on my iPod.

Kai was thrilled to be recognized as we were checking
in, although I told him that it was his orange sequined
scarf and purple pointed cowboy boots that gave him
away.

"Welcome, Mr. Kai," the manager said, greeting us
warmly. "We're so thrilled to have you. We've reserved one
of our best villas." He glanced over at me, smiled, then
added, "We think you will be pleased."

"Um, how many bedrooms?" I asked as Kai kicked me
lightly in the foot.

"Oh, this villa in particular has just the one, miss. I'm
assuming that you are *together*?"

"Yes, yes, we are," I said hurriedly. "It's just always nice
to have a second room to put things in, stretch out."

"Miss, our accommodations are spacious. I'm sure you
will find plenty of room to do all you need to."

The view was sumptuous, overlooking the translucent
waters outside. There was something pure and uncomplicated about the bedroom, with its canopied four-poster

bed covered in spotless white sheets, yards of muslin tied around each pole. For all its simplicity, it was, without a doubt, the centerpiece of the room, as if everything else had been built around it. It looked like it had been designed for genuine lovers, for people to spend all day in, eating off mother-of-pearl-inlaid trays that would be delivered by room service, stopping their caressing only for that.

For Kai and me, it was completely useless.

"You can have that," I said to him, indicating the bedroom. "There's plenty of room for me here in the sitting room." I fully expected him to demur, to insist that now that he had dragged me all the way here, I should have the only bed in the villa.

"Oh, you sure?" he asked, tossing his luggage onto the floor as if to stake out his territory, then pressing a button to call for our private butler. "That's great. I could really use the rest," he said, stretching. "Of course, feel free to come in here whenever you want, maybe take a nap in the middle of the day when I'm not using it."

"Kind of you," I said, shutting the paneled doors between us.

Kai spent most of his time scuba diving with a young mixed-race instructor named Trey, whose last job had been at the Club Med in Bali. Kai had been raving about his adventures beneath the ocean since the first day, citing for my edification how Jacques Cousteau had described the island as one of the top-ten best scuba spots in the world. He and Trey would frolic for hours beneath the sea, shimmying between strands of seaweed and past hordes of luminous, wriggling fish and coral reefs that Kai said were as intricate as carved Chinese mahogany furniture. Down in those depths, my boyfriend was assured that even the longest lens of the most persistent paparazzo would not be able to find him.

I, as always, spent time alone, reading in our room, swinging on the Balinese hammock on our veranda or walking down a sandy beach by myself, picking seashells as I went, just as I used to do when I was a young girl with my Nana in the Mumbai suburb of Juhu. I looked out over the ocean, blue and clear as far as the eye could see, and wondered if my grandfather ever thought of me, the way I thought of him.

Chapter Twenty-four

It was going to be my first trip back to Paris since I had left for New York, and I wasn't quite sure how I felt about it. The city, as magical as it was, represented everything significant that had ever happened in my life. It was my first escape from my family and also my final alienation from them. It was the place where I was discovered and also the one where I discovered that I wasn't the girl I had always believed myself to be. It was the city where, even if I had never acquired the poise and sophistication I had gone there to seek, I had come closer to it than at any point in my personal history. In an odd sense, it would always feel like home to me.

Shazia was waiting for me in the lobby of the Bristol Hotel, her eyes wide and a big smile stretched across her face as she saw me enter, Kai at my side, two valets with our luggage behind us.

"Oh my God!" she exclaimed. "Just *look* at you! What

the hell?!" she exclaimed, her hands on her hips. "You look *fabulous*! Like a movie star!"

I shrugged my shoulders, embraced her, and asked how her mother was doing.

"Fit as a fiddle, would you believe?" she said, her eyes fixed on Kai's exhausted face. "OK, maybe not quite, but she's in a lot better shape than when you last saw her. I guess the fact that I keep coming back helps."

She stuck out her hand in Kai's direction, waiting for him to grab it.

"I'm Shazia, Tanaya's cousin, almost like sisters really," she said, glancing over at me again. "It's *so* great to meet you, I'm *such* a fan!"

"Any chum of Tanaya's is a chum of mine," Kai said, not very convincingly, shaking Shazia's hand. "Glad to meet you; hopefully we'll see you around. Boys, up this way," he said, beckoning the luggage-bearers to follow him up.

"He's tired," I said to Shazia. "We'd better get upstairs. What are you doing later? I have a show at five; you're welcome to come and hang around backstage, and maybe we can have dinner afterward?"

Valentino had asked me and some of the other girls to join him for a post–couture show supper, to celebrate what appeared to be the unanimous thumbs-up given to his collection of frothy beaded gowns and smart city suits. I kissed him on the cheek and told him I had other plans.

Shazia rode along in the limousine with Kai and me to the restaurant, chatting about Birmingham, her eager face watching his. We arrived at Le Martel, in a part of town I had never been to, not even in my earliest days when I was poor and adventurous. The surroundings were shabby and dark, but a friend of Kai's told him that it was absolutely *the* place to be seen in town, and if there was one thing that was evident about Kai, it was that he loved to be seen.

The place was packed—expected during the couture shows—but we had been given a prime table. The girls were already waiting for us—Juliette and Teresa and Karla—their faces expectant, Mathias cool as ever in their midst. I had never before in my life been so thrilled to see a group of people. I rushed over to them, hugging them all, even Mathias, with whom I had always been reserved. They oohed and aahed over my dress and shoes and metallic clutch bag, and I waved off their gushes of admiration, and introduced Kai. The restaurant, previously clattering with post-show buzz, suddenly turned quiet, its patrons looking our way. Shazia, standing next to me, whispered, "Wow, this must be what it feels like to be J.Lo." In the dim lighting from the globe lamps overhead, my friends looked radiant. With all the recent chaos of my life, I realized that now, tonight, I could take a deep breath and just relax. We ordered artichoke hearts and pasta and grilled vegetables, and Mathias insisted on getting champagne for the table, saying he was in a celebratory mood. When a frosted bottle of Cristal arrived, he raised his glass and tipped it in my direction.

"To our dear Tanaya, who has returned triumphant, as we knew she would," he said, his eyes shining in the soft light. "We all miss you, but, *chérie*, you have done us proud." Karla filled a glass for me and pushed it my way. "You *have* to drink a little now," she said. "Even just a sip. We are toasting *you*. We are celebrating all you have ac-complished, against all the odds. It is no time for rituals. You are a grown woman now, a woman of the world. Come, join us. Drink."

I stared at the pale golden liquid, fizzing in its slender vessel, and glanced at the eager, nodding faces around me. There were plenty of Muslims who drank alcohol, I rea-soned with myself. And after everything I'd done, was I even considered a Muslim anymore? Did Allah even care about me now? My hand reached across the table; I picked up the glass by its skinny stem and held it up to the light. Then I turned toward Kai, handed him the glass, and told him to enjoy it.

By the end of the meal I was the only one sober, for which I was very grateful, as I had scheduled a breakfast meeting with Dimitri, the man who started all this, the next morning. I had noticed, as the evening wore on, that Kai had become increasingly sullen. For once, everyone in our presence was more interested in me than in him, and Kai didn't seem very happy about that. While Shazia still wanted to talk to him about recording deals and performing gigs and his adventures on the road, he quickly grew weary of her relentless attention and looked to the others for the same kind of adulation. He didn't find it. They all wanted to know about me, and me about them, and I could tell that Kai felt left out and disengaged, and the more I tried to draw him into the conversation, the more removed he became. By the end of the night, he was checking e-mails on his cell phone. Mathias looked over repeatedly at Kai, then at me, evidently puzzled. I avoided his questioning stare and, as we were getting back into our waiting car, I deflected Mathias's questions about whether or not I was happy.

"He seems to be, how you say in America, a chuckle-head," Mathias said quietly as we said our good-byes. Kai sat next to the window, waiting for me to walk to the other side. Mathias held my hand and kissed me gently on the cheek.

"I'll call you tomorrow," he whispered.

The phone next to my bed woke me up early the next morning, Dimitri's voice deep and resonant on the other end.

"Just to let you know, I'm on my way," he said cheerily, commuter noise in the background. "I'll be there in ten minutes. Hope I didn't wake up Kai." I looked across the living room at a closed door, behind which Kai was no doubt still fast asleep, and was grateful for two-bedroomed suites.

Dimitri looked smaller and stouter than how I remembered him, but was beaming.

"Such a joy to see you," he said, kissing my hand as I sat next to him on the couch in the lobby. "You are more beautiful than before. Success becomes you. And I hear you are in quite the love affair," he said, eyebrows raised, leaving me to wonder if he knew the truth or not.

"My cousin Stavros has, of course, kept me abreast of your many activities and assignments," he said, his trademark formality rising to the fore. "I am delighted at how well you are doing. Yes, of course, Stavros and I benefit financially from your success, but beyond that, I have always felt that you, more than anyone else I have encountered, deserved to have it. And I can see now that becoming a famous international fashion model has not changed you one little bit. Your family would be proud, if they cared to know," he said, shaking his head, the smile momentarily disappearing from his face.

"Anyhow, apart from wanting to simply see you and tell you how proud I am of you, an interesting business opportunity has arisen. Stavros called me about it the other day. I think it's perfect for you. And, if I do say so myself, my instincts as far as you are concerned have not yet been proven wrong."

In my absence from New York, Stavros had received the call that all modeling agents wait for. It was from a film producer in London who was working on an as-yet-untitled movie project, and who seemed to think that I had the right "look" for it.

"But I'm not a trained actress," I said to Dimitri when he told me.

"Who is?" he countered, his smile returning. "How many of the really great movie stars today are really properly trained? Many of them worked hard or were discovered. Now that's happening to you."

It was being pitched as a romantic comedy about a young, white, preppy, uptight banker who falls in love with a gypsy girl from Morocco with rumored terrorist ties—to be played by me. In the mix was also a dunce of an ex-boyfriend who was trying to extricate himself from the mujahideen.

"It plays into every single silly stereotype," I told Dimitri after he had finished recounting the plot.

"I agree, which is why it will get made," he said, smiling. "It is being packaged for the masses, and therefore is a wonderful opportunity for you. Anyway, the reason it is a matter of some urgency is because the financing is coming from Germany, and the producers are doing their final casting in the next few days. They are flying in from Frankfurt tonight and want to see you tomorrow. In principle, the role is yours. It's just a formality, and to see if they can develop some acting chops in you. I've checked the calendar, and you have nothing on after Chanel, so I've scheduled a meeting. And please, leave your boyfriend at the hotel."

Chapter Twenty-five

The drive to Neuilly was shorter than I expected, with less traffic than usual heading out to the Parisian suburb on an otherwise fashion-frenzied afternoon. My hair felt gummy, my eyelashes still clumped together, as I rushed out of the show without bothering to remove any of my makeup, assuming that the casting people would want to see me in my full fashion-model glory anyway. I stepped out of the long gray car and went up a flight of steps that led to a wide podium that flanked the building on all sides. Through the glass double doors and up an elevator were the offices of the law firm that was handling the deal, where the producers were having a meeting that preceded mine, and from where we would be headed to a café down the street to talk. As I rode up in the elevator, I hoped that Dimitri, who was supposed to be meeting me here, had already arrived.

The elevator doors opened onto the foyer of the company, and a pretty receptionist told me to take a seat and wait. After a few minutes, two men—one broad-shouldered and with a full head of dense, wavy hair and the other slight and balding—emerged from one of the office suites, smiling as they approached me, their hands outstretched. The larger one introduced himself as Werner, the executive producer of the movie, which was being unofficially christened *Honey in the Hamptons*, Honey being the name of the girl in question, and a title that sounded like that of a porn film. Werner's associate was Max, whom Werner introduced as "the brains behind the film."

"Shall we go and find a quiet place to talk?" Werner suggested as Max led the way.

As we made our way the few feet toward the elevator, a voice sounded out from behind.

"Wait, you left these behind!"

We all turned around, and I stopped breathing. Walking toward us, holding a sheaf of papers, a tiny pair of gold loops pinched through his ears, was Tariq.

My breath finally returned, but my body felt like it had been shoved into a microwave on high. He stared at me, the smile disappearing from his face.

"Oh, thank you," said Werner, taking the papers out of Tariq's hand. "We can't afford to lose these!" he said, sliding them into an attaché case he was carrying. Then, almost as an afterthought, he introduced us. "Tariq Khan, I am pleased to present Miss Tanaya Shah. I am certain you know of her. She is a famous model, and will most likely be starring in the movie we were here discussing with you." Although Werner was standing right next to me, his words were faint. My eyes were still on Tariq's face.

"Yes, of course; I am familiar with Miss Shah," Tariq said tightly. I had seen that look before, the last time right before I left India, on my grandfather's face at the airport. It was one of disapproval and disappointment, and it always made me sad. There, standing in front of the man I had first come to Paris for a year before, the man I should have married, I suddenly felt naked. Despite the expensive clothes on my body and the brilliant colors on my face and the showy flamboyance with which my hair was coiffed, I felt like nothing but a silly, small girl, simply playing dress-up.

"We're taking quite a risk by putting you in this movie. As far as films are concerned, you're not exactly a name," Werner said, once we were settled within a cozy leather banquette at a nearby bistro. Dimitri had finally shown up, just as we were leaving the office, and nodded agreeably whenever Werner or Max spoke.

I found it hard to pay attention. Since my shocking run-in with Tariq just moments earlier, I was finding it difficult to concentrate on anything.

"So what do you think of that?" Max asked, looking at me, a question relating to a conversation that I had mentally pulled myself out of.

"Yes, of course," I said, clueless about what I was agreeing to, and hoping that it wasn't a nude scene.

"We're in preproduction now and would like to start principal photography in about a month," Werner said, peering at me over his large glasses. "That should give you enough time to get some acting classes in. I don't expect you to win any awards for this, but it should be a little believable, huh? You should be able to engage the audience with more than just your looks. We'll be shooting mostly in New York, so at least you won't be too far from your beau. Perhaps we can talk to him about doing the soundtrack, yes?" Werner continued, looking over at Max again and scribbling a reminder into his notebook.

As I half-listened to the conversation, I could consider only what Tariq must have thought of me.

Chapter Twenty-six

Thär are some people who believe they are born to act. I am not one of them. I found the lessons excruciatingly humiliating, baffled as to how someone could stand up on a low platform in a darkened room, a dozen strangers watching, and make themselves cry. I was amazed at their ability to do so, but when my turn came, I simply stood there and stared out at them, their faces growing more expectant by the minute.

"You need to *emote*," instructed the coach, Genevieve, who had been an actress herself long ago. "You need to be able to access those old hurts, those painful feelings you think are dormant but are festering in your body. Breathe deep; bring them out."

I squeezed my eyes shut and pursed my lips together, looking for all the world as though I were about to have a bowel movement. I thought of the nana who no longer loved me and the mother who perhaps never had and how truly, truly sad I was. I could feel the sadness in my blood, the slight ache that had hovered around my heart for the better part of the past year, covered by layers upon layers of little luxuries and pleasant distractions.

But no tears came, no emoting other than a little sigh indicating that I had chosen to sleep under the pain and to let it cover me like a heavy blanket.

I looked up at Genevieve, her face expectant, like those of the other students in my class.

"I'm sorry," I stammered. "This is not for me. Forgive me for wasting your time."

I returned to my seat, picked up my bag, and walked out.

I was surprised to hear Stavros's voice on the other end of the line. It had been three days since I called him to let him know that I didn't want to be Honey. I had explained to him that after attending a couple of acting classes, it had become patently clear to me that while other models could try their hand at acting, I wasn't equipped to do so. I told him that it would take self-confidence and grit and being naked in the truest sense, being prepared to be devastatingly bad at something and have a dozen crew members on a film set snicker behind your back as a result. It would also require having an ego. And, if I'd discovered one thing about myself, it was that behind the klieg lights and the limousines and the private jets, I still didn't have an ego.

The following seventy-two hours, as a result, were spent doing what Felicia frenetically described as "damage frigging control." Dimitri and Stavros had been working on extricating me from my contract with Werner and Max and dealing with lawyers. I realized that Tariq must have been among them, but elected to think no further about it. Felicia had calls in to her contacts at *Daily Variety* and the *Hollywood Reporter*, and of course Page Six, all of whom had announced my decision to make a foray into film, and who now would be faced with the prospect of announcing my withdrawal.

"We don't want you to be seen as flaky," said Felicia, her cell phone, as always, pressed to her ear.

"No, God forbid," I replied.

So Stavros's voice was an immediate comfort to me, an indication that he was no longer upset. The line was faint, his voice far away. In the background I could hear a woman's voice announcing flight arrivals in French.

"Where are you?" I asked him.

"I'm here, in New York. But there's someone on the phone for you. He called me looking for you, so I've patched you in. Sir, go ahead," he said, replacing the receiver at his end and telling me he'd call me back later.

"Hello, yes?" I said.

"Tanaya? It's Tariq. Tariq Khan."

I gripped the phone tighter and released the handful of M&Ms I had been munching on, which had now left a rainbow of colors on my palm.

"Hello, Tariq," I said, trepidation in my voice. "It's very nice to hear from you."

"I don't have time for small talk," he said. "I'm sorry. I have a plane to catch. I'm on my way to New York, actually. I have a conference there tomorrow. But, if you don't mind, I need to speak to you about something quite urgent. May I call you when I arrive?"

"Is this about the movie? If so, there's nothing really to discuss. I know they are your clients, but it was really stupid and I didn't want any part of it and—"

"It's not about the movie." His voice was suddenly softer. "I shouldn't say this, but I'm glad you dropped out. I thought it was ludicrous from the beginning, but they had the cash, and I was just doing my job. It's about something else, much more important. Give me your number, and I'll call you when I get in, OK?"

In a corner of the Four Seasons Hotel in New York, Tariq was next to me on a couch, his little gold earrings glinting in the soft shine of the tableside lamp on his right. He was as handsome as I remembered—sturdy and strong and kind. In another age, I would have been graced indeed to have been his wife.

But Tariq looked at me as if he were my parent and I was a child who had broken a brand-new toy. He had wanted to see me because he had wanted to tell me, in person, that my nana was crippled, near death. He had been riding in the back of an auto-rickshaw, on his way to post a letter, and a bus had veered through a red light and smashed into the vehicle he was in. He was lucky to be alive at all, Tariq told me, repeating exactly what he had heard from his grandfather. It had happened three weeks ago, but it had taken this long for the news to travel from Ram Mahal in Mahim to Tariq's grandfather in Pakistan to Tariq in Paris, and finally to me, in the Four Seasons in New York, jazz playing softly in the background.

All I could think of was what my mother had said a decade ago, when a conversation turned to surviving loss. My mother's sister Sohalia, one of the beautiful ones, had asked her one time how she had managed to remain so resilient in the wake of being abandoned by a husband when two months pregnant, how she had not descended into bitterness and endless, raging fury.

I was eleven when I had overheard the question. Aunt Sohalia was visiting from Karachi, and she and my mother were shelling peas at our dining table, their heads covered, their hands busy, their eyes on the slimy green pods in front of them. I was sitting close by, reading a comic book, waiting for my Nana to come home from one of his flights. I don't recall how the subject arose, only that my aunt had been angry with her own husband about something and had, in a moment of extreme pique, even considered leaving him. Of course, we all knew she would never do it. She was, after all, a gorgeous and dependent woman, and he was a rich and powerful man, and thus it would always remain.

But the question caused my mother to drop her pea pods for a minute, and to lift her eyes and cast them out toward the balcony.

"It's easy," she said. "You just think of everything you hated about them. You just focus on the absolute worst in their personalities, the most disgusting habits, the things that irritated you to the point of insanity. I was only with Mr. Hassan Bhatt for two months. But there was so much about him I hated. I might have loved him too, but I have forced out of my mind and heart every recollection as to why. I only remember the hatred. That way, I don't feel the pain." Then she calmly shoved her hands back into the white plastic colander and continued shelling.

My mother had rarely been right about things, but she was right about this. I supposed that if I closed my eyes tight and thought about all the things I disliked about Nana—his constant and unforgiving sternness, the gruff way in which he bid me good morning, his habit of pulling out with his bare fingers bits of sticky white rice that lay impacted in his molars—that if I concentrated only on these things and on nothing else, then maybe this feeling of complete devastation wouldn't overcome me, that maybe, just maybe, I wouldn't die from guilt.

"What do you want to do?" Tariq asked as we stood outside his hotel fifteen minutes later, the crush of New Yorkers getting off work gathering around us.

"I don't know," I said, still too dazed to think. "Maybe

go back . . . but how? They hate me." I looked down at my snakeskin-tipped shoes.

"Look, I have a meeting now, but it should be over in a couple of hours. Why don't you come back here and we'll go out to dinner. That is, if it's OK with your boyfriend," he said, lowering his voice at the last word as if he were uttering some profanity. "Let's try and figure something out. You need to see your grandfather. You can't ignore this, you know."

"I know," I said, shaking his hand meekly and walking down the street, where I dialed Kai's number and explained my situation.

"What the crap do you mean you can't come? The whole goddamn world is going to be there!

"This is bleeding crap, you know that?" he bellowed. I had promised him that I would be there, front and center, at a performance he was giving that night at Chimera, a hot new club in SoHo. He was the star attraction and I, apparently, was a nice little extra inducement. In exchange for him showing up and giving an "impromptu" performance, the owner of the club—a media mogul who was branching out into nightlife—would reward Kai with a Louis Vuitton suitcase and just about anything he could fill it with from up and down Madison Avenue. After Kai's gig I was to go up, kiss him, beam at him, and then at the photographers who would be hovering in the background. It had all been planned, and my dress had been laid out. But now, something more important had come up.

Kai sounded irate, as always. I heard him sniffing, although he moved his mouth and nose away from the phone. I was certain it was cocaine, which he carried around in a container meant for talcum powder, and which I hadn't even noticed until our recent spell in the Turks and Caicos. Until then, I'd thought his moodiness was just that.

"Something has come up, Kai. Please understand. It has to do with my family. I need to go meet someone. I'm sorry, Kai. I know it means a lot to you, and I know you'll do a wonderful job whether I am there or not. For all this time, I have never not stood by the terms of our agreement. But tonight, I need some time off. It is just one appearance. I'm certain people won't even notice."

He swore at me again as he replaced the receiver.

While I was dining with Tariq at Da Silvano's, it occurred to me that, apart from Nana, I had never been alone with a Muslim man before. There was, I realized, something deeply comforting about it. Although we were in the middle of a sophisticated restaurant, surrounded by sophisticated people, sitting this close to him, our elbows touching atop the crisp linen tablecloth and our knees just a hairbreadth away beneath it, I felt like I could have been back at home in India, embedded in the security and safety with which I had grown up.

I wasn't sure why he had asked me out. I had thought that we had said all we needed to over tea, when he told me about Nana and the accident, something I had yet to fully absorb. I had gone through the following few hours in a state of restlessness, there but not, conscious of the yellow cabs honking at me to cross the street quicker, the gawks of the people as I walked by, and the smell of beef franks sizzling from a cart. But I wasn't, for those few hours, really in my body at all. I was somewhere else, in my home in Mahim, holding Nana's frail hand as he lay on his bed, his legs lifeless beneath a thin white bedsheet. I forgot, almost immediately, that he was once dressed in navy gabardine, smart little wings on his shoulders, his peaked pilot's cap sitting proudly on his head.

"You want a soda or something?" Tariq asked as the waiter came by to take our order. I glanced at the menu, rattled off a request for some vegetables and risotto, and turned back to Tariq. His hair was curled over his ears, his silk tie loosened around his neck. He smelled nice. He felt reassuring. I realized that despite the way I knew he judged me, I was very happy to be with him.

"So you managed to get away from your boyfriend for a night, did you? From what I've read, you two seem inseparable."

"It's not what you think."

"No, I'm sure it isn't," he replied sarcastically. "Anyway, that's all beside the point," he continued. "What do you think you're going to do about your grandfather?"

"You know they're not speaking to me, right? You know that as far as they are concerned, I'm dead?"

"But you're not. Dead, I mean. Which means that as

long as you have the inclination, you probably need to try and fix this. They are your family, after all. You may think you have it all—famous boyfriend, big job, lots of money. But did your nana never teach you about the importance of the blessings of our elders? That without those, we are nothing?"

He was beginning to anger me. Something in Tariq's voice, the patronizing way in which he spoke to me, was irritating.

"What? Can't handle the truth?" he asked, thrusting his fork into an asparagus spear.

"It's easy for you to talk," I said through clenched teeth. I could feel the anger in my belly, and I was forcing myself to sit on it, to squash it back, to make it retreat. Da Silvano's was no place in which to have a fit, especially with people at neighboring tables looking my way, wondering who this handsome man was, most likely figuring that he was a brother or cousin. Almost in honor of being with him, I was wearing a long-sleeved blouse and fluid pants, a scarf draped around my neck, as if ready to hoist up to my head at a moment's notice.

"It's easy for you to preach on about family blessings," I said. "You have always had them. No matter what you decided to do, you would always have them. Go to law school, go to med school, stay home and become an auto mechanic. Your parents would never have cursed you with Allah's wrath because you are a man. You were *meant* to go out and conquer the world. But if a girl tries to do it, suddenly there are accusations of betrayal and threats of being disowned. I couldn't even walk out of my apartment building without being followed by Nana. But you? You could study in America, work in London, move to Paris, whatever you wanted. Why? Because you are a boy and I am not?"

"It's not that, and you know it," he said, his gaze now steady on mine. "If you had told your grandfather that you wanted to get a proper education, take on a decent career, he might have eventually agreed. Even *I* would have fought for that on your behalf. But what is this? This taking off your clothes for the world to see? This sleeping with a strange white man who plays music for a living? What kind of behavior is that for a decent girl?"

The anger I had been sitting on threatened to erupt. I put down my fork, a clump or beige rice stuck on its end, and picked up my things.

"Wait, Tanaya, don't leave," Tariq said, a look of alarm suddenly crossing his eyes.

I sat down again.

"I didn't mean that," he said. "I must have sounded like your nana there, for a minute," he said, his face softening. "I just want to understand what this is all about. The last time I saw you, you had just left India for the first time, standing there in your aunt's house. I could tell you didn't feel welcome. You were so sweet and shy, and I wanted to hug you and take you away. But you told me how you felt by not saying anything at all. You only got out from under your grandfather's thumb by agreeing to marry me. But once you got to Paris, you were done with that idea. Am I right?"

I pushed my plate away. I suddenly felt ashamed. I had used Tariq, something that had only just occurred to me.

"All I wanted to do was to see the world," I said, my voice breaking. "All I wanted to do was to glimpse some of what my nana had seen, to share life through his eyes. I thought it would never happen. I put it down to teenage madness. But then I saw that movie, *Sabrina*, and I saw Paris for the first time ever in a black-and-white film, and I knew that I should be here. There was something about her in that movie, something graceful and strong. I aspired to that and thought it would happen for me if only I would be allowed to set foot in that city. It was only meant to be for two weeks. But then my cousin Shazia showed me how different my life could be. It wasn't what I planned. But it was what happened. I was praying to Allah that my nana would understand. But my prayers weren't answered, not that time anyway."

"*Sabrina?*" Tariq asked, smiling now, acting as if he had heard nothing but that. "You went to Paris because of Audrey Hepburn?" He laughed. "That's the most ridiculous thing I've ever heard!"

"Don't make fun of me," I said quietly. "I don't expect you to understand. It was something I just had to do."

"Well, you made it to Paris," he said. "But you didn't

have to take it as far as you did. There was no need for the improper behavior. And then, to top it all off, you hook up with a rock star who I am *sure* is on drugs. Were you so desperate?"

Nilu was the only person I had told the truth to. Now I broke the confidentiality agreement once again, telling Tariq exactly what my arrangement had been with Kai.

"So, you didn't, um, *do* anything with him?" he asked when I was done. "You are still saving yourself?"

"Of course," I said quietly. "My life has not changed me that much. Every woman in my family waited until their wedding nights to give of themselves. I will be no different."

The disapproval that had lingered on Tariq's face the past couple of times I had seen him was now gone. His jaw relaxed; his eyes regained their brightness.

"It was a charade," I said to him. "This thing with Kai. My career. I don't know what I was seeking, but in the end, I didn't discover what I thought I would. I never had my *Sabrina* moment. Right now, I feel like I have nothing but heartache."

He put his hand on top of mine.

"We may not have married," he said. "But because of what our grandfathers once had, I would like very much to be your friend."

At home, an hour later, Tariq back at his hotel, I sat on my couch. My high-heeled sandals lay under the coffee table, a red light flashing on my answering machine. It was probably Stavros. And Felicia. And Kai. I didn't want to see anyone.

I went into the bedroom, opened my closet, and pulled out my tattered brown suitcase.

Chapter Twenty-seven

Damn that Page Six. Or thank Allah for it. I wasn't quite sure, two mornings later, as I lay in bed with the newspapers, Felicia at the foot of the bed like a minder in boarding school, her arms crossed in front of her bosom, her left foot tapping on the ground.

"Disaster," she said, shaking her head. "Absolute, bloody unmitigated disaster."

"It's not so bad," I said, reaching over for my bowl of cornflakes. "At least now the truth is out."

Right there, as the lead item, was a little story about Kai, the hot new British rock star, being caught in a rather compromising position with his bass player, a lovely fellow named Jerome, in an alley outside Chimera.

"You know, it's all because you weren't there," she said. "This whole thing could have been avoided if you had just shown up as promised. His career is probably in tatters now. But I couldn't really care less about that. It's you I'm worried about. What is going on?"

"Nothing," I said as I threw off the covers and put my feet on the floor.

"Well, now that Stavros is done fixing the mess you made with those German filmmakers, we can start from scratch. I know I'm your publicist and not your business manager, but a few opportunities have come up that we can look at. You've gone pretty much as far as you can go with your modeling career, so I really do think it's time to move on. You've made it clear that acting isn't for you. You've got the beauty endorsement. So what else? What else shall we do?" she asked, lowering herself onto my bed.

I could see what she was getting at, but at this point in time, my work, my career, this thing I did, was meaningless.

Felicia's eye fell on a photograph that was lying flat on my bedside table. It was the picture my mother had sent to me, the one of her and my father on their sad wedding day, the one with which she effectively said good-bye.

"Who are all these people?" Felicia asked, glancing at it. Her finger rested on top of my mother's semiveiled head. "And who's that? She could be a candidate for *Extreme Makeover*," she said.

"That's my mother," I answered, my voice now brittle.

"Oh, my, I'm sorry," Felicia said, now contrite. "That was really insensitive of me. I think I overdid it with the caffeine this morning, and this whole thing with Kai and Page Six has really gotten me wound up. I wasn't thinking. Of *course* it would have to be a family picture. Why else would you have it? But," she continued, "has anyone ever told you that you look nothing like your mother?"

"Everyone," I replied.

"Anyhoo, back to business," she said, getting up and pacing around the room. "I'm thinking your own fragrance line, you know, à la Naomi Campbell. Or perhaps a really sexy and exotic ready-to-wear collection, something that has haute bohemia written all over it. You're perfect for that kind of look. People would expect it from you. What do you think?" she asked, oblivious to the fact that I was opening drawers and pulling clothes out from them.

"I think I'm done," I said.

"You *can't* leave!" she shrieked. "Not now! Not with all this going on! You've peaked! You're the hottest you'll ever be, especially with the new scandal!"

She was waving newspaper clippings in the air again. She knew that her phone would be ringing off the hook all day today, from *In Touch* and *Star* and the all the entertainment news shows, desperate for a quote or an interview and more insight into the spectacular revelation that one of the hottest men in rock, in a supposedly sultry affair with a luscious exotic model, was, in fact, gayer than Christmas.

"You will emerge from this smelling of roses," she said, her voice now calmer. "You'll have everyone's sympathy. Everyone will be throwing deals at you. You could open any business you want, with as much backing as you need. You could become an empire!" she said, raising her voice to the sky as if summoning some majestic power.

I sat down on the bed again.

"Felicia, if any of this had ever been important to me to begin with, I would be thrilled at what you are telling me right now. If all I ever wanted in my whole life was fame and riches and a beautiful wardrobe, I would be kissing your feet in gratitude. But you've known me long enough to know that this is not what drives me."

"Then what does?" Felicia sat down on the bed next to me. "What's going to get you excited?"

"I don't know," I said softly. "All this time, with all the amazing opportunities and experiences, a part of me has felt dead. There have been moments when I've been absolutely thrilled, like that first time on Pasha de Hautner's catwalk. But mostly, I have been too guilty to enjoy it. I feel as if in claiming my life, I have taken away somebody else's."

"So how long are you going for?" Felicia asked when I stood up again and resumed packing. "You do realize that once you've been out of the public eye for a while, you run the risk of not being hot anymore. A thousand girls will be waiting in the wings, ready to pounce."

"Let them," I said.

Chapter Twenty-eight

Whoever decided to name Mumbai's international airport Chhatrapati Shivaji should maybe have thought about it for a bit longer. In the days when Nana journeyed in and out through the building as if it were his home, it used to be called Sahar—sweet and simple. By the time I finally got around to seeing it, it had been given a name, which while easy to say if a subcontinental dialect was your first tongue, was monstrous to enunciate if you spoke anything but.

I considered this as I heard the American flight attendant try to announce our destination over the speaker, and I smiled at her efforts. I realized then that it had been a few days since I had allowed a smile to cross my lips, so immersed had I been in anxiety over my grandfather. My biggest fear was that he would die right before I got there, which typically happened in many of the Hindi movies I had seen: The heroine makes a mad dash across crowded thoroughfares to see a long-lost and very ill relative, but life leaves him just as she's entering the doorway.

Roll credits.

I didn't want that to be my ending.

Of course, I wasn't quite sure what I was expecting. I knew there would be no open arms to welcome me; of that I could be certain. But I was hoping that my mother would at least let me into the house and stop long enough to listen to me. And that my grandfather would be so happy to see me and would be so appreciative that I had come to him in his moment of need, he would forgive all. That he would stroke me on the head like only grandfathers can, and tell me that both he and Allah would overlook my sins.

The seat next to me was empty, so I put my bag in it and folded my legs under my haunches. I was wearing the exact same outfit I had on when I left Mumbai more than a year before. It was a thick cotton *salwar kameez* in pale yellow, printed with small green flowers. The carry-on bag next to me was the same one I had left with, made from black PVC, bought from near Crawford market while Nana was shopping for vegetables and fruit and *halal* meat. It was three days before my scheduled departure for Paris, and Nana had said that for a parting gift I could choose one thing: that bag, a pair of woven leather slippers, a lightly embroidered woolen shawl, or some silver-and-stone earrings. I had opted for the bag, drawn by the fact that I would be able to put things into it that I had never owned before: a passport, an airline ticket, a pair of sunglasses that Nilu had given me. I hadn't even used the bag after my career began, going instead for the high-priced ones that I was so often gifted with.

An outside pocket was partly open, a piece of paper caught in the teeth of the zipper. I pried it loose and saw that it contained Tariq's phone numbers. It was the note that Nana had shoved into my hand as I got on that plane. The digits looked faded now, the paper grimy with my own fingerprints. I started to crumple it up, to toss it into the empty teacup that sat on the tray table in front of me. I would have no use for it anymore. But instead, I folded it neatly and slid it into my wallet.

Tariq had offered to come with me. That night, at dinner, when I told him that I had decided to fly back to Mumbai to see my family, he said that he was long overdue for a trip himself and would accompany me, that he would spend a few days in Mumbai seeing friends and then would hop across the border to see his own grandfather.

"Something like this makes you realize that they can go anytime," he said, his eyes growing wistful. "I think I should go see my elders before it's too late. I can't let work run my life."

But I had told him that this was something I needed to do on my own, and he had nodded politely and paid the bill. Outside the restaurant, he had shaken my hand stiffly, wished me well, and turned around to head back to his hotel. I stared at him as he went, waiting for something, not sure what. Then, as if sensing that I was still there, he had turned around and walked toward me again. He stood in front of me, one foot away, both of us bathed in the glow of yellow light from a lamp overhead.

"I am very pleased that I finally got a chance to talk to you, and to know you," he said. "I had wondered, all this time, what you were like. In a way, I am sorry that it had to be under these circumstances, having to share bad news with you. But I also know that if it weren't for that news, I would have had no occasion to call you. So, strangely, I am also grateful for it."

I was quiet for a minute, taking in what he said, charmed at his honesty.

"I can see now that my nana was right," I said. "Without even meeting you, he knew what kind of a man you were, based simply on your grandfather's word."

Tariq nodded and shook my hand again. "Tell your grandfather I say hello," he said before moving out of the yellow light and stepping back into the night.

It was growing dusky as we approached. Gray rivers snaked their way through barren land on the outskirts, with urban density intensifying toward the center of the city. Lights started to come on in the ramshackle buildings as the sun slowly set. The plane descended, and the slums came into view, concrete walls separating them from the airport terminal.

The aircraft landed smoothly and taxied straight up to one of the gates. I slipped my feet, now cold and a little numb from the frosty cabin air, back into the ballerina flats that lay under my seat, the only thing I had on that was from my "second life." I picked up my things, covered my head with my shawl, and walked the short way down the aisle toward the arched, open door.

The lines at immigration were backed up down the large hallway. At the far end, there was a special section for flight crews, and I watched as the attendants from my flight, accompanied by their pilots, whizzed through. My grandfather, in his day, must have done the same.

I suddenly felt nauseated as I thought of him again. We were in the same country now, and I was standing on the same spot where I was sure thousands of times in his life he had stood. I could almost feel him near me.

When I finally got to the front of the line, the immigration officer picked up my passport, still relatively new and crisp despite its extensive use. He flicked through the pages, peering at my photograph, and then back at the various stamps that covered its pages.

"Madam, you are off-duty stewardess?" he asked, his eyes appearing red and watery through his scratched bifocals.

"No, sir," I replied.

"But you are unmarried?"

"That is correct."

"So how you are gallivanting to so many countries all by yourself?"

"For my work," I said, taking the passport back and

squeezing past his desk before he had a chance to ask me any more questions.

I went through at least four other checkpoints after that, each officer rubber-stamping the same stamp that the previous officer had given me, slowing down a process that shouldn't have taken more than five minutes and making me yearn for the smooth efficiency of Zurich, the pristine airport halls of Singapore. I had barely been back thirty minutes, yet I was starting to feel frustrated. "I'm in India now," I had to remind myself. "Get used to it."

At customs, they barely glanced at me. It appeared as if the more affluent a person seemed, the higher the likelihood of being singled out for a full luggage inspection, the assumption being that expensive electronics and velvet pouches of jewelry were probably lurking somewhere between folds of underwear and cotton shirts. But in my average outfit, my face free of makeup, my ears and fingers and wrists unadorned, I was nobody, an uninteresting, average woman who was arriving back at her homeland as anonymously as she had left it.

Nilu was waiting outside, pressed against the metal railings that divided arriving passengers from the people there to greet them. She looked happy to see me, almost relieved, but she also couldn't hide the surprise on her face.

"You made it!" she said, throwing her arms around me. "I was thrilled when you called to tell me you were coming back, but for some reason thought you might chicken out at the last minute. But," she said haltingly, "why do you look like this?"

"Like what?" I asked, glancing down at myself. "These are my clothes."

"Yes, I remember that outfit. You wore it when you came to my house to say good-bye the afternoon you were leaving. But I guess I thought you would return in your full regalia, you know, with the sunglasses and the high heels and those skinny-type pants and that sexy blouse you were wearing when I saw you in New York. Remember? I thought you'd come back looking like a movie star. But you look just like you."

"I am me, Nilu," I said softly as we maneuvered my squeaky luggage trolley through the crowds and to where rows of waiting vehicles were lined up. "Which one is your car?"

Chapter Twenty-nine

Our household, like every household in the world, had a routine. And no matter how long I'd been away, or where I might have gone, I would never forget it. There were nuances to my daily life in Mahim that seemed to remain the same day to day, year after year, times when everything would happen concurrently—phones ringing, servants shouting, radios blaring—and then again when everything was suddenly quiet. As mundane as my existence had been, there was a rhythm to it.

I glanced at my watch and worked out where, exactly, my family would be in the cycle of trivial events that made up their days. Dinner was probably over and, this being a Wednesday night, was most likely chicken cooked in *masala* spooned over saffron rice, a *dal,* a *bhaji.* In my previous life, Nana would be standing up, flicking the grains of yellow rice off his white kurta onto the table to be swept up by the servant's wet rag, and then he would strap on his black leather sandals for a quick walk around the building.

"Good for digestion," he would say, standing up to go. "Helps with emptying of stomach in the morning."

Sometimes I would go with him. We would stroll around our floor first, glancing in through any doors that might be open, willing to nod and say a quick hello to any of the neighbors who might be in the middle of their own rhythm. Then we would make our way up the staircase and walk around subsequent floors, Nana repeating that climbing up and down stairs was good for the heart. Mostly, he and I would walk in silence, taking in the slow buzz of activity — of babies crying and children playing and televisions turned on too loud — that marked a day in the life of Ram Mahal, of just about any middle-class building in India that evening.

If Nana could still walk, that is exactly what he would be doing right then.

"I can tell; you're thinking about him, right?" Nilu asked. She was sitting in the back next to me, her hand pressed into the spongy leather seat. "I haven't been to see him since it happened. But the whole neighborhood is talking about it. It's very good of you to come."

"How could I not?" I asked, trying not to cry, trying to hold it all together. "Who knows when, or if, I might ever see him again?"

"It was pretty bad when it happened," Nilu continued, although I partly wanted her to stop. "It was right there, you know, next to that electrical shop with the owner who is always drunk, opposite that place where your mother bought you the rose pink hair clips. We've gone past that area a million times you and I. That's exactly where it happened. The auto-rickshaw was such a *put-put* that it just stopped, right there, in the middle of traffic. There was no way the bus could have stopped in time. The rickshaw-*wallah* died, there and then."

"Please, Nilu, stop," I said, now crying. "It's too horrible to hear."

"I'm sorry," she said. She paused. "But there's one other thing you should probably know. After the police and ambulance came, when they were putting your nana onto a stretcher and taking him to the hospital, they were gathering his things. He had been on his way to the post office to mail a letter. Tanaya," she said, staring at me, "the letter was addressed to you."

As we approached the neighborhood, it felt like I had never left. Mrs. Mehra's School of Domestics sat on the same corner, its billboard a little more faded than I recall, the cheerful face of a woman in a sari holding a teacup and a platter of cookies two shades duller than I remembered it. All the shops were shuttered for the night, but the street activity remained: young men pedaling by on their bicycles, ringing their bells as they went, children chasing one another around big colored sheets that flapped from clotheslines. The slum dwellers squatted on the pavement, begging for coins from passersby, or rummaged through the big open bags of trash for dinner scraps.

I stared out of the car window, Nilu silent by my side, as we pulled up outside the building. A couple of lights were on in our apartment, but there was no sign of anyone, although I was certain that both my nana and my mother would be home. They were always home.

"I'll come in with you, make sure everything is OK," Nilu said as she was about to instruct the driver to wait. "You never know how they are going to react after everything that's happened."

"I appreciate the thought, but I should go alone," I said. "I got myself into this, and I'll have to get myself out."

Still, I was immobile, silent and staring for a few minutes, almost waiting for a sign that I was supposed to step out of the car, down the narrow entryway into our building, then knock on its blue painted door.

"I wonder what was in that letter," I said to Nilu, both of us knowing I was stalling for time.

"Me too. After telling you repeatedly that you were dead to him, he goes and writes to you. And on the day he decides to mail it . . . oh, it's just so sad . . ."

"Stop it, Nilu," I said. I took her words to be my sign. I kissed her on the cheek, thanked the driver, opened the door, and walked into the building.

The smell hit me as soon as I was inside—that combination of fried cumin seeds and boiled sugared milk, tainted by a tinge of raw, untreated sewage. I had grown up with that odor living in my nostrils, and now I inhaled it deep, as if to affirm the fact that I had finally come home.

I stood outside the door. There were voices inside — my mother's and the cook's. I didn't hear my nana. The door next to it opened, and the teenage twin brothers who lived next to us peered out, looked at me in astonishment, began whispering to each other, and went back in.

Within an hour, everyone in the building would know that I was home.

I raised my hand and knocked. I felt dizzy and nauseated. It must have been pure terror, but having never felt that before until then, I didn't initially recognize it. There was no response from behind the door, so I lifted up my hand and knocked again, this time harder.

"Kaun hai?" I heard my mother's voice, enquiring who it was. I remained silent, thankful there was no peephole.

"Kuch kaho!" My mother demanded that I speak.

"Ma," I said, softly, imperceptibly. "Ma, *main hoon.* It's me."

I know she didn't hear, because I heard her muttering about being disturbed, thinking I was one of the neighbors needing to borrow some *ghee* or a pound of *moong dal* to soak for breakfast.

I heard the door unbolt, a light switch coming on. Her expression went from exasperation to something I had never before seen. Shock, outrage, incredulity, perhaps a combination of all these.

"Tum," she said quietly. "You?"

I had known she wouldn't hug me, or even smile. But

I didn't think she would slap me, not after that night twelve years earlier when she unleashed her fury on me and promised never to do it again. My cheek reverberated, hot and stinging, while I stood there and stared at her, my hand on my face. Then she lifted her hand again, and this time struck me on the other side. The cook had appeared, standing behind her, a stained dishcloth slung over his shoulder, his mouth open. He had lost another tooth.

There was no sign of Nana anywhere—not even his slippers beside the door, where they always were.

"Ma, I've come home," I said, tears gushing down my prickling cheeks. "I'm sorry for everything. I just wanted to see you and Nana. Please, can I come in?"

Her face was gray, the black mark on her forehead creased and darkened.

"If you are here, then you are a ghost," she said, her teeth clenched. "Because you are dead. May Allah forgive you for your sins. But we never will. You go, and never come back here again."

She tried to slam the door, but I put my foot over the threshold so it stopped at my toes.

"You can hate me," I said. "But I've come to see Nana. I know about the accident. Please, Ma, let me see him. Before it's too late."

She stared at me, the anger in her eyes now turning to something else. Something like hatred. "It's already too late," she said, banging the door shut.

My tattered brown suitcase stood humbly on the ground next to me, outside the place I had called home for nineteen years.

I couldn't move. I couldn't think. I didn't know where to go or how to feel. There were tears, I knew, clogged somewhere in the back of my brain, but it was as if they couldn't find their way out. My cheeks still hurt, and my toe smarted from my mother slamming the door on it. I wondered if Nana was dead. The way my mother had spoken, that was certainly how it sounded. Just thinking of it made me feel like I had been kicked in the stomach. It can't be, I rationalized. If that was the case, Nilu would have known. She would have told me. Unless, of course, it had only just happened, right before I got there, just as it always did in the Hindi films. I shook my head, tossing out those thoughts, praying that my mother simply wanted to hurt me, knowing that it worked.

My first thought was to call Nilu. But I was suddenly shamed and humiliated and thought that even the comfort of a good friend wouldn't help me. I thought of everyone in my life—all the friends I had acquired far away—and how none of them could help me. I thought of turning around and going back in, but the look on my mother's face told me that she felt as anguished as me. I couldn't do that to her anymore.

I stooped over to pick up my suitcase, thinking of which hotel I should go to for the night before considering what I ought to do next. I also needed to cry, but wanted to do it away from this building with its nosy neighbors and gossiping grandmas. I just needed to get out of there.

A male voice sounded behind me, whispering my name. It was the cook, a row of teeth interrupted by big spaces, his dark face almost invisible in the night.

"Kya hua?" I asked, wondering what had happened and why he was out here, talking to me.

In his Hindi-Marathi mix, he told me that Nana was alive, and at home. He wasn't well, but he was a little better than he had been yesterday, which was significantly better than a week before that. He still couldn't walk, and probably never would. He was weak, but he was eating. In a drug-induced delirium, right after the accident, Nana had asked for me. He had called my name out loud a dozen times. He had said he didn't want to meet Allah until he saw me again.

"Main kya karun?" I asked our cook, wondering what I should do.

"Kal," he said.

Tomorrow.

Chapter Thirty

Growing up, I had always longed to go to the Hotel Sun 'n' Sand. Even the name mesmerized me. It made me think of tall frosted glasses of fresh coconut juice, tiny pieces of pulp floating inside the otherwise clear liquid, served by uniformed waiters to long-legged foreigners who sat by the pool. I would imagine platters of *bhel puri*—tiny twigs made from chickpea flour tossed with spiced rice crispies, boiled potatoes, and coriander and heaped with a dollop of tart tamarind sauce—that would lie untouched on buffet tables as rich people perused the other offerings. I used to close my eyes as we drove by in the back of an auto-rickshaw, my nana and I, on our way to somewhere far less grand and much more mundane, and I would wish to simply sit in the air-conditioned lobby for a minute or so, to stare at the wealthy locals who came there to dine and drink and dance. At its prime, on the sun-swept shores of Juhu, there was nothing else like it.

With the palm trees outside my balcony, now encased in the pale darkness of early night, I could have been anywhere in the world. It felt odd to be at home, in my birthplace, and not be in Ram Mahal. There was something illicit about it. As much as I had longed to be here all those times I had driven by with Nana as a little girl, it saddened me tremendously to have to be here now.

But I slowly unpacked, ordered up some room service, said my prayers, and waited for the sun to rise.

With all the traveling and time-zone hopping I had done in the past year, I still wasn't used to jet lag. When I finally awoke, it was past eleven, and my head still felt heavy. For a second, I couldn't remember where I was, nestled under this strange comforter and atop the starched white sheets, searching for the pillow that had gotten dislodged during the night and was now by my feet. I sat up, looked around, felt the silence of the room, and started to cry.

According to my rough calculations, it was late in Los Angeles. But I knew that Shazia would be up. She had told me that she rarely went to bed before one a.m., sitting up to watch TiVo'd episodes of *The Ellen Show* and Jon Stewart before finally falling asleep.

She answered immediately.

"I saw this weird number on my caller ID," she said, her voice excited. "Where you calling from?"

"Home. India home, I mean," I said.

"You went back there? Holy crap! What's *that* like?!"

I told her what had happened the night before, and she let out a low, disapproving sigh.

"I knew it," she said. "I knew they would act like heathens. They don't deserve you."

"Please don't speak about them that way," I said quietly. "They are my family. They told me what would happen if I disobeyed them, and I went ahead and did it anyway. I deserve what has happened to me."

"Wow, they've really done a number on you, haven't they?" I heard Shazia turn down the volume on her television, the laughing and applause in the background slowly fading. "If there is one thing I've learnt since I left home, left the culture I grew up with, is that our parents don't have the right to tell us how to be. They should simply be grateful that we've turned out OK, with no drug addictions or criminal records or illegitimate children running around. Here, in America, a man wouldn't *think* of disowning his granddaughter because she wanted to pursue a modeling career. Hell, I don't think he'd care. He may even be proud of her, would boast to all his friends on the block. There's one thing you need to get through your head, Tanaya. You shouldn't be groveling for their forgiveness. They should be groveling for yours."

I heard a knock on the door. Breakfast had arrived, and I used that as an excuse to hurriedly hang up.

The clerk at reception who had checked me in the night before had recognized me. He had done a double take, looking up again from his computer screen, a grimace of satisfaction spreading across his face when I told him my name.

So I shouldn't have been surprised when, as I was stepping out of the hotel at one thirty in the afternoon, several photographers were lined up outside the building, cameras in hand aimed at me like weapons. A young woman probably my age, standing on the sidelines, a multicolored cloth bag slung over her shoulders, came racing toward me as soon as I emerged, a small tape recorder tucked into her hand.

"Miss Shah! Miss Shah!" she yelled out, trying to catch me as a I hailed a cab. "I'm with the *Times of India,* lifestyle section. Miss, what brings you back home after all this time? Are you working on any deals with local companies? And why are you staying here instead of at your family home?"

I had one leg in the taxi, but stopped. I remembered Felicia's advice about always being pleasant to the press, whether I was in a rush, or in a bad mood, or even distrustful of them. "The least you can do is smile and wave," she had said. "But never be rude, and never walk away without giving them something."

"I'm here for a family visit, that's all," I said, forcing a smile. I waved at the rest of the cameras, smiled again, thanked them for their interest, and folded the rest of myself into the small black taxi.

❊   ❊   ❊

In the bright light of day, Ram Mahal looked imposing. Now, under the glare of the sun, I could see its former glory hidden beneath layers of dirty rain stains and pigeon droppings.

I was standing on the other side of the building, scared to be directly in front of the balcony, certain that my mother would emerge there at some point that early afternoon, to dry her hair on one of the rough pink towels that she always used.

Lurking in the back, shuffling from one foot to the other, I felt like a criminal. I hadn't really planned what I was going to do or say, only that I would try and get in again, past the fury of my mother, relying on the assistance of the cook.

Just then, I heard a car honk behind me. I turned around and saw a taxi pull up right next to me. The door opened, and out stepped my aunt Gaura, suitcase in her hand.

"Tanaya, you're here!" she said, her face beaming, her arms wrapping themselves around me before I had a chance to move. I sunk into her embrace, our two silver-streaked heads bowed together.

"When did you arrive?" she asked, releasing me. "Why are you standing here? I've come to see Nana; he's very sick, you know."

"I know." I began crying again. "I tried to see him yesterday, right after I flew in, but Mummy wouldn't even let me through the door. They really hate me. So I went to a hotel."

"What nonsense!" she said, now frowning. "I never understood why they treated you so badly. You are one of our own. They might not have agreed with your choices, but you are a grown woman now."

I stepped back and looked at my aunt with gratitude and surprise. I realized then that I had never really known her, despite our closeness when I was an infant. I had never taken the trouble to visit her in Pakistan or even to reply to the letters she would write to me, when she would always enclose a leaflet of shiny stickers or a dried flower she had made in an arts and crafts class. I had set her correspondence aside, reading and then ignoring it, seeing it as nothing more than a formality between an aunt and her niece.

"You have always been like a daughter to me, Tanaya," she said then, smoothing down my hair. "I should have called you, and I am so sorry I did not. I think I knew that you would always come home and make things right. In the meantime, Nana and your mother refused to even let your name come up. It was very sad," she said, shaking her head. "But, my girl, you are home now. We will do what we can to bring us all together again."

She didn't bother knocking on the blue painted door. It was ajar, as it always was this time of day, so the cook would hear the cries of the vegetable seller as he made his way down the corridor, a large circular basket of tomatoes and parsley and okra atop his head. Aunt Gaura simply pushed the door open, announced her presence, clutched my hand, and walked in.

"What is *she* doing here?" my mother asked, emerging from the bedroom we once shared, her black hair wet and stringy against the polyester gown she always wore at home, a sprinkling of fragrant white talcum powder visible around her neck. The cook emerged from the kitchen, smiling at me.

"She was waiting outside, *bechari*," Aunt Gaura said, referring to me as the "poor girl" that I felt like I was. "How are you treating her like this? Has she harmed anyone? Yet even so, she has come to ask for forgiveness."

"Ma, I just want to see Nana," I said, my voice cracking, looking toward his closed bedroom door.

"He doesn't want to see you," she spat out. "He's in poor shape. Seeing you will kill him."

"That's not true," Aunt Gaura said. "He's been asking for her, and you know it. Don't lie. Come," she said to me, taking me by the hand again like I was a child and this was my first day of kindergarten. "Let's go see your nana." She set down her suitcase, walked toward his room, and pushed the door open.

Had I not known he was still alive, I would have thought I was looking at a corpse. He was half his weight, shrunken and bony beneath a white cotton sheet. His eyes were closed, his skin pale, a gray stubble roughening his cheeks and chin. His silvery hair, lighter and thinner than I remembered it, stood straight up on his head, disheveled and uncombed. Lying there, he reminded me of a broken fluorescent tube light, all brittle and skinny and shades of gray, the monochrome broken up only by a black thread worn as a necklace, a small silver talisman hanging off it. On the table next to the bed was a copy of the Koran and his reading glasses, dusty with nonuse. Bottles of pills and syrups cluttered another table, a large glass jug of water next to them. The room smelled of urine and antiseptic, like the hospital where my grandmother had died years earlier.

I stood there as if glued to the floor.

"He's sleeping," Aunt Gaura whispered to me. "He needs his rest. At least you have seen him. Come, let's have some tea and return later."

When I was a child, my most profound fear was losing my grandfather.

Every time a plane crashed somewhere in the world — even if it was a charter jet in the interiors of Russia, something I rationally knew my nana would have nothing to do with and was nowhere near — I couldn't sleep until he returned safely to our home, his peaked cap nestled on his bedside table. Each time I put on the television and the news came on, I was anxious until the sari-clad newsreader, her *bindi* as big and bright as the moon in the center of her forehead, moved on to sports, knowing then that there had been no plane crashes in the world that day.

And even after Nana had retired and he was always there, in the next room, the pages of his newspaper rustling in the mid-afternoon breeze, I don't think I ever stopped worrying about him. Every time his temperature went up a few degrees, or he complained of a headache, or perhaps was afflicted by a bout of indigestion after a particularly rich meal, my thoughts would always run to the extreme: It was cancer, a brain tumor, he was about to have a stroke.

It only occurred to me much later, that the dread with which I held my nana when I thought I was about to lose him was the same dread with which I encased him when he was well and sound and happy. I feared him; I feared for him. There was, I realized, nothing about our relationship that wasn't based on fear.

"You have to know how much he loves you," Aunt Gaura said. We had returned to my hotel, and were seated at the coffeeshop, cups of *masala chai* in front of us. "You have to know that no matter what you did, there wasn't a day when he didn't think of you. At the same time as he was cursing you, he prayed for you." She sighed and readjusted her headscarf. "I will never understand that man. I will go to my grave, and he to his, without ever truly knowing him."

She paused for a moment and glanced around the coffeeshop, her eyes falling on the smartly dressed people at adjacent tables. Even in her simple light orange cotton *salwar kameez* she was a stunning woman, heads turning toward us when we walked in, us looking more like sisters than aunt and niece.

"You have done well," she said, putting her hand on mine. "When I was your age, I was married with a child on the way. I would never have been able to afford even a cup of tea here, much less to stay here on my own. You have broken every rule of our family. But somehow I cannot judge you. I cannot be like the others. I fed you from my own breast when you were just days old, and I cannot kill you off in my mind like the rest have done."

I started to cry softly, deeply moved by my aunt. She reached over and put her hand on my head, atop the Shah streak, and smiled at me softly.

"If I really think about it, I guess I can understand why Nana is the way he is," I said. "He is from another generation, after all. He is an old-timer in every sense," I said, now laughing. "But to see the fury on my mother's face—it shocked me. I had never seen such a thing. I had never seen much of anything on her face." I stirred my tea, watching as the swirls of milk dissolved into the caramel-colored liquid.

"It pained me to see how she was with you," my aunt said, her expression now sad. "I couldn't understand how a mother couldn't love her child."

I thought back, for a second, to Zoe, my first roommate in Paris, the short-haired American girl who had given birth to a daughter that she had never wanted either. Perhaps it wasn't so uncommon after all.

"When your mother saw how beautiful you were becoming, she almost turned against you," my aunt continued. "She wanted you to be like her. She began to see you as a stranger. And when she realized how much your grandfather loved you, and how close you were to him, she put herself in the background of your life, concerning herself with whether the vegetable basket was full and that your school fees were paid on time. But she never knew how to really be a mother to you, did she?" my aunt asked, looking at me with such tenderness that I wanted to cry.

Aunt Gaura's words were shocking to me, even though she was telling me something I think I always knew. I pushed my chair back as if I needed to stand up and go somewhere, when I really had nowhere else to go.

"*Maasi*, tell me something," I asked. "My friend Nilu told me that Nana had the accident on his way to the post office, that he was going to mail something to me. What was it? Do you know?"

Aunt Gaura scooped another spoonful of sugar into her tea. She then lifted up her head and stared straight at me.

"It was a letter from your father."

Chapter Thirty-one

Spandau Ballet was playing in the elevator as I rode up back to my room. I recognized the song from a fashion show I had done in Rome a month earlier, where the designer had resurrected the trends—and the music—of the 1980s. He had put me in a lime green jacket with big padded shoulders and a peplum waist, and had given me a tiny miniskirt to wear with shiny pantyhose and high-heeled pumps. He had crimped my hair and clasped dangling gold earrings onto my lobes. When I was ready, staring into a mirror backstage and preparing for my turn to head out to the catwalk, the young dresser whispered in my ear that I looked like a "poor Bangladeshi Ivana Trump." I had laughed, too carefree to really be offended.

As I stood outside my room, searching for my key card, I thought back for a moment to those days when my life was an endless flurry of fittings and parties and limo rides and photographers and hundreds of hours spent in fancy airport lounges where all the food was free.

Even when I was famous, I never felt it. And now, being a lifetime away from all that, it didn't even feel real anymore. I barely gave a thought to what had happened with Kai and his career, and Felicia and her neuroses, and Stavros and the wife he pretended he wasn't married to. They all seemed like characters I had read about in a book long ago, part of a life I had never really sought out, and that I was now happy to leave behind.

I was just about to pull down my door handle when I heard the pleasant ring of the elevator, the upward arrow turning red, footsteps coming down the hall toward me, quicker than usual.

"You're a hard girl to find."

I looked up.

"Your cook told me you were staying here." Tariq looked happy and radiant.

"What are you doing here?" I said, surprised but not displeased to see him. "I thought I asked you not to come."

"You did indeed," he said, still grinning. "But I was on my way to Pakistan to see my own grandfather, just as I told you. And my office wanted me to take a meeting with some financiers in Bollywood. So here I am. I went by your place hoping to see you, but got your cook instead. So it didn't go well, then?"

"No. Quite badly, actually. But my mother's sister, Gaura *maasi,* is helping me. She's the only one in my family who understands and who actually doesn't hate me."

"I don't hate you, if that makes a difference," he said, the overhead lights bouncing off his shiny black hair, his tiny earrings trembling with the slightest of movements.

"You've been very kind to me," I said. "I don't deserve it. Right now, I can only think of my nana, of getting him to see me, to know that I dropped everything and came back for him. I'm supposed to go back later this evening, when he will hopefully be awake."

"Sounds good," Tariq said. "I've finished my meeting and don't have to leave until the day after tomorrow. So please, let me come with you."

This time, he was awake. This time, there was nobody to tell me I couldn't go in, that I couldn't touch the hand of the man who had loved me more than anybody else ever had. Aunt Gaura silenced my mother again and waited outside the bedroom door, making awkward conversation with Tariq, who clutched on to a bottle of mineral water.

There was no anger in my nana's voice, and in a way I wished there had been, because that would have told me that at least he had some energy left, that all his senses hadn't been diminished and deadened by his accident.

"*Beti,* you've come," he said, his voice low and guttural yet consoling.

"I'm so sorry, Nana." I was sobbing now, relieved that at least I was able to see him before he got any worse, and even more relieved that he didn't hate me like he said he did.

"I'm so sorry for everything that's happened. I don't know what came over me. I don't know why I had to leave. I should never have. Please, I beg you, forgive me," I said. I placed my head on his chest, like I used to do when I was a little girl. This time, like he did then, he put both his hands on my head and stroked it. When I sat up again, tears coursing down my cheeks, he turned his head slightly to look at me, his eyes a little wider.

"I did not understand what you were doing," he said. "You have brought disgrace to the Shah name. After you left, I could never again walk through the neighborhood without feeling ashamed. But," he said, pausing to lick his lips. "I am not angry anymore. I am too weak to hold on to grudges. So if you have come here for my forgiveness, then your trip is not wasted. You have it."

It was what I thought I wanted to hear. But now that he had said it, I was still unsettled. He wasn't angry anymore, but that look on his face was still there, the one shadowed with disappointment and despair. He looked at me like I was the child who had burned down the family house by mistake, unable to be blamed but a source of endless regret anyway.

My grandfather might have still been alive. But I knew that I had already lost him.

I said nothing to Tariq on the way back to the hotel. He had wanted to know what had happened, what had been said. But my head was a mess, my brain clouded with misery and confusion.

"Through the door I saw him put his hand on your head," said Tariq finally, as we were approaching the hotel. "That must have made you very happy, that he is not cursing you anymore."

"Not being cursed is one thing," I replied. "But having blessings, that is something else." I bit my lip. "I'll never have those blessings again."

The sun was a brilliant burnt orange, getting ready to settle down for the night. The outside of the hotel was relatively quiet, just a few taxis like ours pulling up at the taxi rank, small pockets of people standing around, making plans. The drinks-and-dinner crowd would be arriving soon.

We made our way around the building to the poolside, which was now empty except for a staff member replenishing towels in the cabana in anticipation of the next morning. We sat down on the edge of a deck chair, facing each other. I was twirling the corner of my *dupatta* around my index finger, pulling the fabric tighter and tighter until my fingertip turned red, then releasing it again and feeling the grooves that had been furrowed into the skin.

Tariq reached out and put his hands on top of mine to stop my nervous movements.

"I'm not quite sure I know what you're all wound up about," he said. "Things have gone well. Better than expected. You're back in your family's good graces. Well, maybe not your mother. She still seems pretty angry. But with time, even she will come around. You are her flesh and blood, after all."

I nodded, touched by Tariq's desire to help me feel better. He stood up and turned around, easing himself down next to me. A soft ocean breeze came up off the beach and whispered gently around us. His skin was fragrant, his hands warm. He felt strong and steady, and all I wanted to do was to rest my head on his shoulder.

If I had listened to my grandfather, Tariq and I would be wed already.

If I had listened to Nana, I would be living with this wonderful and kind man in Paris, the wife of an esteemed lawyer, making plans to bear children of our own, my silver hair on the pillow next to his.

I should have listened.

He put his arm around my shoulder and pulled me toward him. The cabana boy was gone now. We heard the keys of a piano tinkling in the lobby as people settled down to drinks and hors d'oeuvres.

"It's weird how things turn out," he said softly, leaning his head against mine. "From the first time I saw you, standing in your aunt's house in Paris, I knew there was something special about you. I thought of you a lot after that." He held my hands in his. "I just want to be with you all the time," he said. "That's why I keep popping up in your life, finding reasons to see you." He laughed sheepishly. "I'm not going anywhere," he said. "I want a future with you."

I let his fingers caress mine, nuzzled my face in his neck. His lips first fell gently on my cheek, colliding with a single tear that had trickled down. I turned my face toward his and let his mouth find mine. His eyelashes fluttered against mine, we were that close. I flashed back to the three other men I had kissed in my life—a boorish British photographer who had forced himself on me, a married man in St. Tropez who had made me feel secure, and a gay rock star who forced his lips to touch mine only for the cameras.

This, now, with Tariq, felt completely right.

There were some things, I decided, I should have listened to my nana about.

Chapter Thirty-two

Shazia had text-messaged me.

YR FMLY IS TXIC, she wrote. *U DNT ND THM NYMORE.*

After everything *she* had been through, I was surprised she didn't understand. She called me later, telling me that if I didn't "get my butt back to New York," my career would be over and I would be "nothing more than a contender for *The Surreal Life.*"

"Shazia," I said quietly. "I really love you, but I think you watch too much television."

Tariq was leaving for Karachi in the morning, but would be stopping by in Mumbai again before flying back to Paris. We made plans to meet in a couple of days, to decide what to do next.

I was elated. Despite everything that had gone on with my family, I was starting to feel stirrings of joy again. I had never been in love before, had never even been remotely interested in a man. Having grown up with a mother who had had nothing but anguish because she had tried to conjoin her life with that of a man, I was surprised that I was even thinking this way. I was not quite twenty-one — still, in my mind, too young to be married. But Tariq, I knew, would not be like my father.

My father.

Aunt Gaura came by the hotel the morning after Tariq and I kissed, bringing with her the envelope that Nana had been holding on his way to mail to me the day he almost died. The small brown envelope had a tire tread mark on one corner, blood stains on another, and was now creased and wrinkled.

After my aunt left, I opened it up tentatively, aware that I had never before even touched something that my father had touched.

Inside was a thick black cotton thread, from which dangled a silver crescent moon and a small five-pronged star next to it, the symbols of Islam. There was also a letter, written on three sheaves of yellow-lined paper, the handwriting neat and precise, and looking remarkably like my own, as if that was the one thing I had inherited from my father.

My dear Tanaya,

You must be wondering why, after twenty years, I am now and only now finally writing to you. Please know immediately that the fact that I have not written previously is no indication of how much I have thought of you. For if it were, I would have written every day.

I have seen from the newspapers that you are living far away, in a foreign land, alone, doing something that has contravened our culture and your upbringing. While it would be easy for me to judge such actions, I have stopped myself from doing so, as I have not been present these past two decades to understand what has motivated you to take such a drastic step for your life, what has compelled you to leave home and expose yourself to the world the way you have.

Knowing your grandfather as I did, I am certain that his disappointment in you must be so profound that he is not even speaking to you anymore. Therefore, I wonder if this letter will ever reach you, as he and I are no longer in touch either. It would be an act of Allah indeed if we three split souls can, through this one letter, come together for the briefest of moments. That is my prayer.

But in the assumption that this note, and the accompanying taveez, finds its way to you, there are a few things I need you to know.

You might have been led to believe that I was a ruthless and heartless man, abandoning your mother so soon after our marriage, at the start of your blossoming in her belly. In the first place, and contrary to what she may have told you, I did not even know that she was with child until after you were born. And by then, I was too ashamed to step forward and think of claiming you.

But of equal importance is my need for you to know the truth about my marriage to your mother. I did not leave her. She left me.

I know this might shock you. It shocked me. After all, despite my disappointment when your mother lifted up her veil on our wedding day, when she was not—as I was led to believe—the bearer of the kind of beauty that the Shah family is known for, I had made a vow in Allah's presence to honor my union with her, and I was committed to doing so. I will not lie; our marriage was not a happy one. I felt duped by your family. Your grandfather needed to marry your mother off, and chose to hide the truth about her until it was too late.

But still, I stayed with it. I was not the most even-tempered or good-natured of husbands, I will confess. But I told her that we would do our best. In the end, you must understand, it was not I that hated your mother. It was she who hated herself. I tried to make her feel comfortable, if not loved. I tried to make her feel that despite everything, she still had a place in the world.

But nothing worked. And one day, after morning prayers, she packed her bags and left.

I have been motivated to write to you now because my brother died recently of cancer. He was only two years older than I, and in seemingly good health until the cancer attacked his liver. He was gone within three months. I realized then that death can come upon us at any time, and I did not want to leave this earth without you knowing the truth, that I could have been a father to you had I been given the chance, and that maybe if I was, you would not have felt the need to leave your life and seek out another just as your mother did.

243

*You may do with this information what you will. My
address is above should you like to write to me, and please
know that I would be very happy to hear from you. I never
remarried, have had no other children. Your name, I will say
in closing, is lovely and appropriate, redolent of more than
beauty. Your grandfather raised you indeed as a child of his.*

*Salaam Alaykum, my dear Tanaya. May peace be
with you.*

Yours,

Hassan Bhatt

It was all too much. Losing the love of my grandfather,
gaining knowledge of my father, letting myself slip into
love with the man I had once used as an exit from my life.

During the two days that Tariq was in Pakistan visiting
his own nana, I barely left my hotel room. Nilu came to
visit a few times, and we had lunch in the hotel café, she
still enamored of my ability to sign my name on a piece of
paper and have it be charged to a room for which I, and I
alone, would ultimately pay.

My aunt Gaura also stopped by, bringing me chunks of
goat simmered in tomatoes, coriander, and cilantro, and
pliant wheat chapattis—everything kept warm in the confines of a stainless steel tiffin. She said she was concerned
about me, thought I might starve, not quite realizing that I
had the ability to feed myself.

"How is he?" I asked her during one of her visits.

"Actually, I think a little better. Perhaps seeing you has

helped him. I hope you will come back again, now you know that he doesn't hate you."

"And Mamma? How is she?"

"Still angry. Still sad. But I suspect it has nothing to do with anything you've done. I suspect that, instead, she sees you as the woman she never was."

I showed her the letter from my father, and the look of astonishment that appeared on her face as she read it mirrored my own.

"We never knew," she said, putting the pages down when she had finished. "Your mother always made it sound like it was his fault, like it was he who wanted her to get out. She couldn't tell the truth, even to us."

Tariq's plane was touching down close to midnight. I had taken a hotel car and was waiting for him outside the airport.

I saw his handsome head bobbing through the crowds, an overnight bag weighing down his right shoulder, his laptop computer bag in his other hand. He was gazing straight ahead, not expecting me. I buoyed myself for the great welcome, a surprise airport reception for the man I loved. I smoothed down my hair, licked my lips, and made my way to the far end of the railings, where I could almost collide with him. I couldn't wait for him to scoop me up, a bright beaming smile on his face, maybe twirling me around in his arms like they did in all the Hindi films. I couldn't wait to smell his aftershave, to feel the strength of his warm hands pressing into my back. I couldn't wait to start a life with him, away from all this.

He looked at me, and the expression of surprise on his face stayed just the way it was, for a little longer than it should have. There was no bright, shining, "I'm so thrilled to see you" smile. There was no enveloping hug. Just a stony face, quiet and contained.

"Tanaya, what are you doing here?"

"I came to see you, of course. I really missed you." I caressed his arm with my hand. He moved it away.

"Tariq, what happened? What's the matter?" Dread was growing in me.

"This is no place to talk," he said, glancing at the chaos around him. "Come."

The Sun 'n' Sand never looked more forlorn. In the dead of night, the palm trees were quiet, the food hawkers, usually parked on the street outside, now long gone.

We made our way back to the pool, attracting looks from the staff at the reception desk and the bellhop. I didn't care who saw us, or what they thought. Tariq was still silent, as he had been on the ride over, ignoring my impassioned pleas to speak with me, glancing at our car driver as if he were from the FBI and Tariq were an internationally wanted criminal.

We sat down on the same chairs we had used a few nights before, the night we had kissed.

"OK," Tariq said. He was wringing his hands. "Here's the thing."

I drew a sharp intake of breath, promising myself I wouldn't let it out fully until Tariq had spoken his mind, until whatever lumbered in the ether between us was gone.

"You know, I really think you're fabulous," he said, his eyes cast downward on his hands. "You're gorgeous and sweet and kind. The other night, after what happened between us, I was certain that I was falling in love with you."

He was looking straight at me.

"But," he said. The rest of the words tumbled out. I heard them, but couldn't take them in. He talked for a full five minutes, pressing his hands together, then biting a fingernail, looking up at me and then down at his shoes again. As he talked, I felt my heart breaking. There were tiny fissures at first, deepening into cracks, finally forcing my soul open.

I didn't move. I didn't speak.

And when he was done, I realized that I hadn't properly exhaled yet.

Chapter Thirty-three

This time I was in jeans, a pink cashmere sweater hugging my curves, kitten-heeled mules on my feet. I stared out the window as the plane flew over the Indian Ocean, my ears still blocked from the takeoff, but open enough to hear a baby crying several rows behind me.

Tariq's grandfather had disapproved.

It was as simple as that. His grandfather, best friends for decades with my own nana, had told Tariq that under no circumstances was he to even consider a future with me. Any type of association, he had dictated, was now completely out of the question. I had been tagged as a "woman of poor reputation," not just because I had left home against my grandfather's wishes, but because I had spent the better part of the past year wearing bikinis and plunging-neck dresses in front of cameras held by strange, lustful men.

"It's not like *I* don't understand," Tariq had said to me the previous night on the deck chair, his voice plaintive, his eyes wishful. "I get who you are, and what all that was about. I know that behind all the show and clothes and makeup, you're this really simple girl. I'm OK with it. But my nana . . . he is like your own—of another time, unable to comprehend modern life. He has forbidden me from having anything to do with you. I'm sorry, Tanaya."

And he had gotten up and walked away, leaving me sitting there, the wide plastic bands of the chair pinching into my thighs.

The first flight back to New York that I could get a seat on was the following evening. Before I left, I went to say good-bye to Nilu, stopping by her house, driving past mine on the way. I turned toward the ground-floor apartment and saw my mother sifting a tray of rice on the balcony, picking out tiny stones and pieces of gravel and tossing them onto the street, her face blank and empty.

Nilu had cried, hugging me tight, knowing that if she ever wanted to see me again she would have to fly to New York.

"I don't think I can ever come back here," I said. "Not after everything that's happened. I can't spend the rest of my life waiting for them to accept me."

"I understand," she said, kissing me on the cheek. "Here, for the plane." She reached under her mattress and pulled out a copy of *Teen Cosmo*, the most recent issue, stashed in the same place as when we first looked at them years ago, when I was still innocent.

❖ ❖ ❖

Felicia was thrilled to see me. She called Stavros and suggested a "get-together," so they could come up with a "POA"—a Plan of Attack—about what I should be doing next. The next round of shows was about to start, castings soon to begin. A car maker was willing to throw a big chunk of cash my way to film a commercial. There were a few offers for paid appearances at nightclub openings. And Playboy couldn't wait to talk to me about disrobing for a spread they wanted to call "Behind the Burka." I blanched at the thought of it, knowing that even I would draw the line at centerfold nudity.

"You've been out of the news for a week," Felicia said, stubbing out her cigarette. "In this business, that's a friggin' lifetime. Oh, by the way, what happened at home? Everything good? Family all copacetic with your career?"

"Yes, fine," I lied.

Back at my apartment, which Stavros had held on to in the hopes that I might return, my mail was stacked atop the coffee table. I quickly went through it, tossing out the catalogs and the mailers until I came across a postcard. The picture was vaguely familiar. I flipped it around and saw that it had been sent from Parrot Cay, in Turks and Caicos. Kai's handwriting was compacted into a few square inches of space.

T. I've absconded! Trey and I are in love. He's going to keep teaching scuba diving, and I'm going to write music. It's blissful. I don't care what people say anymore. I'm done with the charade. Love you lots. Thanks for everything. K.

With feigned enthusiasm, I attended all the meetings that Stavros had set up and sat down for a couple of magazine interviews that Felicia had arranged, where the reporters only wanted to know about my life in the wake of Kai leaving me.

Otherwise, throughout all the small talk and discussing of business details with Stavros and Felicia, I kept my sorrow at bay. Each time Nana's pale, ashen face appeared in my mind, I would squeeze my eyes shut, forcing the images out. Each time I reheard Tariq's words of good-bye echoing in my ears, I forced my attention back to the subject at hand, to contractual details and scheduling, something I actually had some control over.

"You know, this whole thing with Kai—him leaving you and shacking up with a male lover in the Caribbean—it's just *such* a blessing," said Felicia. "The press is all over it. You're the gorgeous girl that he left behind. *He's* the one that looks like a jerk. But what a great opportunity for us. And hey, it's not too soon to start thinking about a rebound, about who we can set you up with next. But maybe this time, we should find someone who swings your way, huh? You want to give the sex thing a try? Add a little sizzle?"

I stared at Felicia and thought that, for once, maybe she had a point. I had been alone long enough.

"I'm happy to try and meet someone," I said. "Maybe

it's time I lived in the real world, not the one my mother lived in. New York is not Mahim, is it?"

Felicia ignored me and started going through her Rolodex.

His voice crackled through static and background noise.

"I'm on a plane," he said. "On my way to you. It was last-minute. I just wanted to know that you were there. I would have waited, even if you weren't."

I asked him what he wanted, why he was calling. I was angry at first, then in tears, standing on a corner of Lexington and Fifty-fourth, waiting for the light to change so I could cross the street, being pushed and pummeled on all sides by office workers on their lunch break.

"Please, Tanaya, don't make the same mistake again," said Tariq. "Don't do it. Look, we're landing in five hours. I'll call you."

He stared at everything in my apartment, as if expecting to find more hints of debauchery, more windows into the life of bacchanalia he thought still I led.

He looked surprised that there were no mirrors on the ceiling, packets of cocaine on the windowsill, a library of porn tapes on the bookshelf. He looked pleasantly surprised that there were fresh flowers on the dining table, that family photos were still everywhere, at the smell of *suji halwa* rich with cardamom, my favorite dessert, emanating from the kitchen.

"I still don't know what you're doing here," I said to him. "You can't just keep showing up like this. It's not fair to me. You made your feelings very clear to me when I last saw you in Mumbai."

"They weren't my feelings. They were my grandfather's."

"Same thing," I said sourly.

"I was in Los Angeles the other day, another meeting. I saw a copy of the *Star* at the supermarket checkout, that picture of you on the front, holding hands with that famous new actor. I thought you were done with all that, Tanaya. I thought that after seeing your nana you were going to lead a more respectable life. I figured that maybe, if you calmed down, stayed out of the press for a while, maybe embraced Allah again, my grandfather would reconsider, and we may perhaps have a future together."

It occurred to me as he was speaking that I had never gotten angry before. Never really, really angry. I had had my moments of irritation and despondency and mild aggravation. But now, as I looked at Tariq's face, still handsome as he beseeched me to "change my ways," the rage that had simmered away in my belly for what was probably most of my life was finally getting ready to pop.

I picked up an empty vase and threw it in his general direction.

"Stop judging me!" I screamed. "More than anyone else in my life, *you* should be the one to understand! *You* are the one that walked away from me that night in Mumbai, leaving me sitting alone by an empty pool in the middle of the night! Where was I supposed to go? What was I supposed to do? How *dare* you lecture me! You are *not* my grandfather! And now you're telling me that you flew across the country so you could tell me about what to do with my life? What gives you the right? Who are you to me? Nobody! Not anymore! Not the day you decided to listen to your grandfather and pay more attention to what an old man has to say than to how it would make me feel! Now please, just get out!"

The look of alarm that had appeared on Tariq's face at the start of my rant was still there when I was done. Even I was taken aback by the depth of my anguish, the realization that Tariq, standing before me in his slim black suit, represented my nana, and my mother, and the father I had never known.

He said nothing. Instead, he picked up his laptop, turned around, and walked out the door.

It was five p.m. when he left.

I figured I would never hear from him again. I figured that he was the last remnant of an old life that I had to let go of, following my grandfather and my mother down a sinkhole of people who would never even try to understand me.

But at six the next morning, after a night of fitful sleep, I picked up the phone when it rang. His voice was immediately contrite, lacking the bravado he had always displayed, the superiority with which he had spoken to me.

"I'm supposed to be leaving later today," he said, sounding as if he, like me, had had a bad night's sleep. "Please, just give me five minutes. Please."

Central Park was busy, joggers checking their watches, mothers calming fussy babies as they walked, looking desperately as if they, like me, needed to go back to bed. The reservoir sparkled under the early morning August sun, pigeons coming to rest on its edges, foraging for food in the dewy grass.

Tariq was in sweatpants and a T-shirt, his eyes slightly red, his hair uncombed. We walked in silence for a while, then sat down on a bench, pushing aside a brown paper bag that had been left there by its previous occupant.

"I've been an asshole, haven't I?" he said, looking at me. "I don't know what it is. I think that I'm this man of the world, and then I go back home and all that goes out the window. It's like I become my grandfather, seeing the world through his eyes. It's pretty pathetic."

"It is," I said.

"But you've got to admit, you don't exactly make it easy on me. Or on yourself. I mean, look at what you've chosen to do. It's unconventional, even for the most liberal of Western families. And here you are, from one of the oldest and most reverential religions of all time, where women are shielded and protected, and you're letting it all hang out. I mean, you have to admit, it would be a stretch for anyone to accept."

"I thought all I wanted to do was to see Paris," I said, looking down at my hands. "I think I knew I was running away from something, but at the time, I wasn't sure what it was. That life, the one that Nana had in his mind for me, it wasn't what I wanted. Not at nineteen. And then everything happened, and I went along with it, loving it as I went, making these choices that would once have been incomprehensible. There have been struggles, but so much of it has made me, well, *happy*. My heart is ready now, for whatever might come next. It wasn't before, you know."

I looked up at him.

"But that's how it started. I just wanted to see Paris."

"And you did. And you will again, I'm hoping." Tariq smiled. He leaned over and kissed me on the forehead, wiping away a tear that had escaped from my eye.

"What are we going to do?" I asked.

"Don't worry. We'll figure it out," he said, putting his arms around me, both of us turning to gaze at the gleaming reservoir.

Chapter Thirty-four

We don't celebrate Christmas in our religion. But in Paris, you couldn't not. So there was a big tree in our living room, more for decoration than anything else, reaching almost to the ceiling, with that fresh pine smell that I had only ever read about. Tiny red lights sparkled on the lush green branches, a stack of presents beautifully wrapped and beribboned piled underneath.

The sun had set already. But I loved the evenings, when we would light a fire and cuddle up in thick knitted sweaters and drink from a large pot of herbal tea.

I glanced around the room, which glowed from the lights on the tree and the fire in the hearth and the warmth in Tariq's eyes. He was looking through his CD collection, his back toward me. Next to him, on a long wooden console, was our wedding picture from three weeks earlier at Tariq's home, just he and I with a mullah and a smattering of friends. Shazia was there, my only link with my old life, the one who had started all this. She had hugged me as the mullah recited prayers, reminding me that she had, long ago, tried to convince me that everything would turn out OK. Next to the picture was a folder containing flyers announcing a charity I had set up, a group for Muslim youth living in Paris who were confused about their cultural identity. Through it I had already met girls like the one I once was, girls who didn't know where they belonged, who felt alone, clashing with a culture they didn't know how, or whether, to embrace.

Tariq found the CD he was looking for. It was Edith Piaf, and her classic rendition of "La Vie En Rose." He slipped it into the player. I smiled at him across the room and moved toward a mahogany desk that nestled close to the window. A tasseled lamp shone brightly onto it. The windows were closed, but beyond I could see the dark surface of the Seine running its course through the city, the lights in other households shining in the distance.

I sat down at the table. I closed my eyes for a second and imagined Audrey Hepburn when she was Sabrina, in her white nightgown, sitting down at her table, in that scene that would never leave my memory.

I pulled out a letter pad, picked up a fountain pen from Tariq's collection, and began: *"My dearest Nana."*

And I wrote until the sun came up.